1500

BY

LEAH TOOLE

1500

Also by Leah Toole

The Tudor Heirs Series

I – The Saddest Princess

…

II – The Haunted Queen

…

III – The Puppet King

…

IV – The Forgotten Prince

~

The Rose and the Pomegranate

To

The thriller lovers.
I hope I make you gasp at least once…

DAY FIVE

PROLOGUE

With her son's latest postcard in her hand, Mrs Peñasco sits down at her dining room table in Madrid to eat her lunch.

Her maid brings a tray, serves her, and Mrs Peñasco picks up her silver spoon and carefully tests the soup's temperature on her top lip before taking her first tentative sip.

As she reads her son's cramped words on the back of the postcard, telling her all about his and his new wife's adventures in Paris, a fly buzzes by her ear.

She swats at the creature absentmindedly, her eyes continuing fixed on the postcard.

She flips it over to take another look at the picture of the Eiffel Tower on the front, smiling as she does so.

Mrs Peñasco then turns her attention back to her soup, eager to dig into her meal when she stops and screws up her wrinkly face.

The fly is frantically wriggling about in her bowl, kicking its spindly legs, drowning itself in its efforts.

Frustration at her ruined lunch takes over then but is swiftly replaced with an intense rush of horror.

Something is wrong with her son. She can feel it.

She looks back down at the poor fly – now dead in the warm liquid – her appetite and her serenity completely shot; for Mrs Peñasco has had one of her premonitions, and she knows that her son is likely already dead.

DAY ONE

<u>Ethel</u>

"A bunk bed, Edward?" I say as I giggle into my hand. I turn to my new husband, "For our honeymoon?"
Edward grabs me and pulls me to him before pressing his lips to mine. His moustache tickles my nose.

"This is one of the best rooms," he reminds me, "The best we could afford, anyway."
I smile up at him, wrap my arms around his slim waist.

"In any case," he says, his brown eyes hooded with desire, "I'd happily share a single bed with you."
I manage to breathe a laugh before his mouth finds mine again, a boyish grin brightening his tanned face.
I always knew that I would marry Edward. Ever since he proposed to me when I was fourteen.
I don't remember when we first met, but Edward had been a colleague of my father's for some time and so, when he asked for me to marry him I immediately said yes despite our thirteen year age gap.
But it wasn't like that. Edward is a kind man. And he promised to wait until I was of age.
And so, for the past *six years*, I had been not so patiently waiting for him, while he worked himself to the bone as a brick layer to be able to afford our wedding and this wonderful honeymoon. Of course, once I was old enough to find work myself, I too had been saving towards this new chapter in our lives. Working as a cleaner in the hotel back in Norwich was not the job I'd always dreamed of, but I was hopeful to find something more fulfilling in the years to come. Maybe in a few

years' time, after Edward and I have had one – or maybe two – babies –

"What do you say we try it out, the bed?" my new husband mumbles playfully into my neck now, the hairs of his moustache against my skin making me squeal.

I turn around in his arms, press my back against his chest, and survey our small room: the dresser in the corner, the window overlooking the water. This little space would be our haven for the next few days. And who knows…maybe we will even conceive our first child on that very bunk bed.

Thomas

My stomach is in knots, and I feel nauseous as I reach my arms into my uniform's jacket.

I'm not ready to return to work, not really. But I have to. I have to think of my boys. They need me to be strong.

When Jennie got sick, the doctors said there was not much they could do. We'd had plenty of forewarning. Plenty of time to adjust to the reality that she would die.

But even three months after her funeral, I still have mornings where I wake up and reach across the mattress to pull her to me, only to find that she is not beside me, her side of the bed cold and still. Just like her.

But for my boys, I will go on. I have to. To provide for them. Even if I'm slowly dying inside, missing Jennie as I would a vital limb, on the outside I make sure to put on a brave face.

When I left the boys at my sister's place this morning on my way to work, I gave them each a coin and made them swear not to spend them until my return. William, who is just five, beamed excitedly at the shiny money in his hand, while Thomas – my namesake – was a little less impressed. At eleven, he is not so easily distracted from his mother's recent passing.

I only hope that we will all one day recover from this tragic loss.

Now, as I stand watching people arriving from all over the world, I wonder if anyone else is feeling as rotten as me on this glorious day. Honeymooners, businessmen, families, we all have our stories. All of us with our own reasons to be here.

And my job was to make sure that things would go smoothly.

Michel

"*Allez, garçons,*" I say in our mother tongue, so that my four, and two, year old sons can understand that we are in a hurry.

"Where's mama?" my eldest – named after me, Michel, but who we call Master: a nickname that stuck – asks, his little voice sounding distressed.

I usher them into our room, drop our bags against the door with a sigh.

"Don't worry about mama," I tell them, "She will find us later."

The room isn't big, but it has all we need for this quick getaway. There is a bunk bed, a desk with a mirror, and a slim sofa in the corner. I eye the couch suspiciously, my brows furrowing at its questionable size. I would have to sleep on the floor.

"Look, papa!" my two-year-old, Edmond, cries, climbing the steps to the top bunk, "Look what I can do!"

He grins at me, his chubby cheeks like two red apples, bright with excitement and adventure.

"Very good, Mon," I mumble, offering him a smile as I reach for our two small bags and plonk them on the desk.

There will be no need to unpack during our stay, I think as I eyeball the dresser by the window. *This way, at least, we will have a quick escape at checkout. Less fuss.*

Master and Edmond screech loudly beside me then, the two of them rolling about and tickling each other on the top bunk.

"Be careful, you two," I mumble in French as I take a seat on the sofa, one of its springs immediately digging into my left buttock.

I shift over to the other side, shaking my head in annoyance.
This is meant to be one of their better rooms!
I sigh as I watch my boys wrestling, their giggles filling my heart with joy.
It may not be the best of the best, but it would do for what I had planned for my family.

It is so big!

I didn't realise I'd said it out loud until my brother, William, who is two years older than me, threw his head all the way back and muttered, "Uh-huh!"

"I bet there will be loadsa places to hide!" I say excitedly, elbowing him in the ribs.

William clicks his tongue, "I always find you anyway," he says, his mouth doing that annoying smug thing that he does.

I stick my tongue out at him and reach over to pinch him, when Mother nudges us forward.

"Come on now, children," she says, her normally soothing voice sounding on edge, "No dawdling."

As we hurry inside, our father, who had been following behind, suddenly steps in front of us. He sticks his stumpy finger in mine and William's faces.

"*Don't* run off," he commands, his blue eyes wide and his thick Scottish accent strong. He means it. "Stick wi' us at all times, do ye understand me?"

I nod my head, my blond hair falling into my face.

William doesn't say anything, and I roll my eyes at him when Father straights up and turns around.

"This way, please!" someone calls.

I look up to see a man in a uniform waving his arm at us to follow him. There's shuffling behind us, someone bumps into me.

I grab onto my mother's soft hand and hold tight, frightened suddenly of getting separated from her. I hadn't realised just how many people were checking in at the same time as us. It hadn't looked like quite so many when we were all outside.

My parents hurry to follow the man, and I widen my strides so I can keep up.

"Down this way, ladies and gents," the uniformed man says. He winks at me as I walk past, a friendly smile on his face. I like his cap.

And I just about manage to smile back at him before being dragged along behind my mother.

Victor

"*Mi amor,* are you ready?" I call as I stand by the door of our suite, adjusting my wristwatch.

"*Si!*" I hear my wife's voice from the other room, the sound of her heels growing louder as she approaches.

Maria turns the corner with a smile, her thin lips bright red, my favourite colour on her. Her olive skin and dark brown hair always look good with a splash of colour.

Her head is at an angle and her hands by her ear as she adds the final touch to her ensemble.

"What do you think?" she says as she gives me a quick twirl.

I lean in to peck her on the cheek, "*Maravillosa.*"

I think back to the swimming costume she was wearing just two hours earlier, how the wet, black fabric had clung to her petite frame as she'd stepped out of the heated indoor pool. It had been the first thing Maria had wanted to do upon our arrival: to take a dip in the onsite swimming baths. And I wasn't about to deny my gorgeous new wife such a wish, especially when it meant I got to reap the rewards of seeing her stunning body dripping from head to toe, the sight of the water running down her bare thighs as she'd emerged having been the most wonderful of payments. The sex that followed thereafter, the cherry on top of the cake.

Maria takes my arm now, bringing me back to the present.

"Don't wait up, Mina!" she calls over her shoulder to the maid.

I don't turn to see her reaction. Mina has been like family for so long, I trust her completely. Especially given she has been with us through each step of the way during this eighteen-month long honeymoon across Europe!

This part of the trip was not planned however, completely spontaneous. Maria and I had been exploring Paris, in fact, when we decided we wanted a change of scenery.

My mother was not best pleased. She thought we'd be coming back, settling down, after Paris. But Maria had had other ideas. And I didn't want to disappoint her.

I grin down at her as we walk through the carpeted hallway to the dining area.

The Restaurant is à la carte and we were expected to book a table in advance, of course. I had made sure to reserve the best seat in the house, at the very centre, so that all could see how beautiful my wife is.

Descending the stairs, we see other guests, all dressed in their finest, also heading to the Restaurant, no doubt.

I take a quick look around, content as I do so that none of the other gentlemen's wives look quite as glamorous as mine. I can't help myself, but a smirk pulls at the corners of my mouth.

"Table for two?" a thick set lady dressed in a maroon garb asks the head waiter at the entrance.

The waiter looks apologetically at her, "It is fully booked," he confesses, and the lady gasps dramatically at the announcement.

I shake my head at Maria as we walk past, who purses her lips at me to stop herself from laughing.

"*Nouveau riche*," she mumbles at me disparagingly.

The waiter who directed us through the restaurant presents us with our table. I nod at him in thanks and pull my wife's chair out, catching a glimpse of her cleavage as she takes her seat.

I bite my lip in anticipation for later, an evening of fine dining and excellent wine no doubt leading to a wonderful show of thanks in the bedroom.

The waiter hands us the daily menu.

"I'll take the salmon with hollandaise sauce," I tell the waiter after just a moment, "My wife will take the same."

Maria does not argue. It is partly why I fell in love with her.

As we await our meals, sipping our champagne, I take a look around the room.

Almost every table is occupied, all of them set up beautifully with silver utensils and stylish centre pieces. I approve, of course. Only the best for my wife.

"Look, look," Maria whispers then as she lifts a delicate hand to tug at her left earlobe, pretending to fumble with her earring as she sneakily points towards a couple at the entrance.

I follow her direction and raise my eyebrows, "It's him!" I say excitedly.

"And his little wife," Maria adds as she turns to look the other woman up and down.

"Should we call them over?" I ask, looking around to see if another table near us is free.

Maria turns to me, her thin eyebrows almost meeting at the middle with the intensity of her frown.

"And besmirch our reputation?" she asks rhetorically, "She may try to hide it, but we all know what she is carrying under than dress."

I had not considered it.

"Besides," Maria says, turning away from the couple as they were led to the far corner of the restaurant, "It appears he, too, is still trying to hide her away. Why else would he have booked the corner table?"

Maria was probably right, though I didn't care much for gossip.

I did not know the man that well, but being one of the richest men in the world…one heard stories. The rumour mill never did stop turning in these circles.

But from the looks of his new wife, it appears these new rumours, at least, were completely true.

"I wonder how he even has it in him," Maria mumbles as she shrugs one delicate shoulder, her thin eyebrow raised.

I look at her, give her my full attention.

"Well," she says nonchalantly, "With his new wife being younger than his eldest son…how does he have the stamina?"

"John is only forty-seven," I add in the wealthy man's defence, as though he could hear me.

"But she is – what? – twenty?"

"Eighteen, I believe," I correct her as I sip my champagne.

Maria shakes her head, "Scandalous."

I don't disagree with her. It *was* all a bit scandalous. But then our salmon arrives, and I no longer care about other people and their sex lives.

As long as mine never becomes a topic of discussion.

DAY TWO

Ethel

I wake up to the feeling of Edward's hand on my hip.

"Good morning," he mumbles, his voice groggy from sleep.
I only smile at him, conscious of my morning breath.
He chuckles, "I don't care," and he plants a kiss on my tightly closed lips.
I squeal and push him off me, forgetting that we were squeezed together on a single mattress. He falls to the floor with a loud *thump* and I cover my mouth in horror.
But to my relief he is laughing as he sits up.

"I guess I deserved that," he mutters, rubbing his elbow.
We get up and brush our teeth side-by-side at the sink, Edward flashing me mischievous glances at every opportunity.
He looks good first thing in the morning, bare chested and carefree, with only his white shorts to conceal his dignity.
A grin spreads across my face as I wipe my mouth with the towel, and I just know that my cheeks are burning bright.
Last night had been…incredible. More than incredible. Despite our confined sleeping arrangements – or perhaps because of it – we had the most wonderful time.
It has been only four days since we got married, and yet somehow it feels as though we have never been apart.
I don't like to think of those years – the six we spent at a distance as we laboured and saved to be able to afford this life together. Edward had gone off to America to find work, had said they paid better over there. I had accepted it, of course. I was only fourteen at the time, and he knew best.

But waiting for him to return had been difficult, made more difficult still when my father had suddenly died, and my mother depended on mine and my older siblings' incomes to make ends meet. The fact that I was saving for a better life – a life away from her and all that I knew – was not reason enough for my mother to be lenient. I had lost half my savings to supporting the family by the time Edward returned to Norwich to rescue me. And it really had felt like being rescued.

"What are you thinking about?" Edward says now as he approaches me from behind and wraps his arms around my waist, his face nestling into my neck.

"You," I admit, feeling like a shy schoolgirl at the thought of him. Us. Last night.

I turn around in his arms, "What do you say we explore a little after breakfast?"

Edward nods down at me, though his eyes – and his hands – are roaming over my nightgown.

"Or…" he suggests, meeting my gaze.

I bite my lip, the intensity in his stare rendering me completely powerless.

He leads me to the cramped bed, and I let him, kissing me as we go. But not before I cast one quick look out our window, as a lone seagull flies past.

Thomas

I hadn't liked the idea of being away from my boys for almost two weeks, but the job paid well.

In fact, with my expert knowledge and education, mine was one of the highest paying jobs available.

I was one of thirty-five men entrusted to keep things afloat, to keep things from turning ugly. Which was a lot easier said than done when dealing with such a large resort.

"Has the fire been put out yet?" I hear my gaffer, Joseph Bell, call to a group of my colleagues as he strides towards them.

I turn back to my work, shutting out their response. That wasn't my area. Besides, small fires were to be expected, especially when everyone was a little on edge. The beginning of the season always being a little hectic.

I think of Thomas and William as I work, and of what they might be doing. My sister Matilda, their aunt, will take good care of them while I'm away. Of that, I'm sure.

I am the youngest of my parents' litter, while Matilda is the eldest, a whole fourteen years older than I. Between me and her, our parents had three more children. But Matilda had always been my favourite sibling, for she had been like a second mother to me.

Born in the market-town of Carrickfergus, Ireland, my siblings and I had – what I believed to have been – a fantastic upbringing. We didn't have much in terms of grandeur, but our hearts were full. Even if, some nights, our stomachs were not.

But that is one small improvement I wished to make for my own children – for their stomachs to always be full.

It was why I forced myself to accept this position so soon after Jennie's passing. Even though I would rather do anything but. But it's not just about me, is it? As a parent, you're no longer just *you*.

And I can't expect Matilda to look after them every time I'm feeling too grim to take care of them. I'd dropped them off at hers one too many times in the weeks that followed Jennie's funeral. When they had needed me the most, I had abandoned them. But after this job is done I'm putting my own feelings aside. There's no room for my misery in this.

My boys are all that matter. They are all that keep me going.

Michel

The feeling of something wet and warm splashing all over my legs wakes me with a start.

"*Urgh!*" I exclaim at the sight and smell.

"Papa," my youngest mumbles from the bunk bed, "I feel sick."

"Yes, Edmond," I say, "I see that."
I stand up sheepishly, unsure what to deal with first. I stand there, looking around for something to wipe the vomit off with, the sight of half-digested carrot chunks making me queasy. Edmond groans on the top bunk.
I quickly grab the nearest towel and clean up as best as I can, fully aware that I'm in need of some sort of bowl or bag to catch the next bout of heaving that may occur at any moment. Failing to find either, I haul my two-year-old out of bed and hold him over the sink, just in time for him to spew the rest of last night's dinner into it.

"I don't feel good, papa," he cries, holding his tummy, then, "I want mama!"
I swallow hard, "Mama is not here right now," I tell him as I lovingly wipe his mouth.
Edmond cries harder, before another heave interrupts him.

"What's happening?" Master's voice sounds from the bottom bunk. I look over at him rubbing his eyes.

"Go back to sleep," I tell him gently, though the sun has already risen, "Mon is sick."
Master only nods sleepily and turns back around. He was always a good sleeper. I think.

In front of me, Edmond's teeth are chattering. Probably shock.

"It's okay," I soothe, smiling at him encouragingly, "Do you think there's more?"

Edmond shakes his head with effort, and I bundle him up in my arms, careful not to further aggravate his upset stomach.

I lay him back down on the top bunk, tucking the sheet around him.

"I want mama," he mumbles again as I stroke his little back. I *shush* him gently and his eyes begin to close again, "I know, *mon bébé*."

It's what his mother always calls him, so I know it is what he needs to hear right now. Sadly, it is the only thing of his mother that I can give him.

Because she isn't here with us. And we'll never see her again.

Catherine

My brother William and I are staring into each other's eyes, willing the other to blink first.

I know I'll win, because his eyes have already gone glassy. Any second now he will lose.

But then he blows a puff of his stinky breath at me and I flinch, my eyes fluttering in response.

"Cheat!" I yell across the long rectangular table, ready to pounce on him and smack him across the head. But he only laughs.

"Kids!" our mother's voice calls, interrupting our fight before it even began, "Not now."

I huff back into my red-leather upholstered chair, "But –"

"Catherine Nellie Johnston…" our father full-names me from beside our mother. His voice is low and his tone unthreatening but the full-naming in itself is enough to put me in my place.

"Sorry," I mumble, to which William grins smugly at me.

I'll kick his sorry butt later.

The bowl of oats fails to appeal to me. I pick at my food but eventually push it aside.

I heard there was a pool, though I doubt we'll be allowed to go…

"Can we go play?" I ask Mother, my bottom lip jutting out. Maybe she'll say yes, even if to just have some peace from us. She looks over at Father, a question in her eyes. He was in charge, of course. We all knew it. Though we always made sure to show Mother respect by asking her first. Besides, Father was much more likely to say 'yes' if Mother asked.

Andrew Johnston was not someone you'd want to cross. I'd seen him turn all kinds of shades of red at people throughout the years.

If someone bumped into him in the street – accident or otherwise – they'd be on their arse before they'd had a chance to apologise. We had the bailiffs come round our home once, to repossess the radio after Father had failed to pay some bill or other. They took it, of course, but not without a fuss, my broad-shouldered father standing in the doorway throwing insults at them until they left. They returned the next day with five others in tow, and that time they made their way inside without a word from Father. He knew they meant business. But they didn't find our radio, though, not until three weeks later when they finally thought to dig up the garden.

Father would've rather seen the thing rotting away under the earth than to hand it over to them without a fight.

But when it came to our mother, Eliza, he was a softy.

He sighs heavily now before looking around, "Go on then," he says, his Scottish accent still strong though he's lived in Croydon for years, "But not up the stairs."

I grin at him and Mother, bouncing excitedly, "We won't!"

William grabs my hand, and together we race away before Father could change his mind, eager to explore our unknown surroundings.

We speed past the other guests, some of them families, like ours, who had kids. But we weren't here to make friends. Not today.

We run out of the dining room and turn a sharp left down the slim hallway, our feet *thumping* loudly on the wood flooring.

I don't know why, but I start laughing. It feels freeing to be running again after being stuck in our stuffy room all night.

Can't we crack a window? I had whined at Father last night when I had felt like I couldn't breathe, William's farts stinking up the place.

Does it look like we can crack a window? Father had answered, to which I'd hopped off my bed and taken a look for myself. But he had been right. The window was sealed shut.

Victor

I decided to let Maria sleep in, to recuperate from last night. I wish I meant that she was exhausted from an intense night of lovemaking, as I'd hoped she would be. But she'd been too sloppy for that.

Dinner had turned into drinks in the lounge, and well…let's just say she'd had one too many. It might have been embarrassing if she wasn't so gorgeous. But her beauty expunges all her other, less attractive, qualities.

Though I had expected some gratitude from her at the end of such an opulent night, I am still a gentleman…and having sex with someone who was not even conscious was not exactly my idea of a good time.

I take one last look at her as she snores lightly in the double bed, then I close the door behind me with a *click*.

I always felt that the best thing to do after a night of drinking was to exercise first thing in the morning. Sweat out the toxins. That's what my father always used to say.

I find the gym easily, the signs leading me down a hallway and into a well-equipped onsite fitness centre.

There's no one else here apart from the instructor, who raises his head from the newspaper he was reading and offers me a friendly smile.

"Do you need assistance?" he asks me, to which I only shake my head.

I do not like to be watched and supervised while I exercise.

To my surprise, he returns to his magazine, unfazed. I'm glad for it.

I'm not a muscly man, not really. I'm not interested in building up my body. But I take my health very seriously, and for me to feel good in my own skin I like to work each of my limbs just so. The body is a machine. And in order for that machine to work effectively, one needs to make sure to oil its parts properly and frequently.

I'm on the rowing machine, finishing my set, when a man walks in.

"Do you need assistance?" the instructor asks, as he did when I entered.

The man stops and opens his mouth, unsure, before shaking his head and cautiously walking towards the weights.

I watch him from the corner of my eye, certain I have seen him before, but unable to figure out when or where.

He appears to be in his fifties, which I find a strange age to start going to the gym. I say 'start going' because he clearly has no idea what he's doing with those weights.

I look over to the instructor, wondering if he's noticed that this man is doing his muscles no favours at all and will likely displace his shoulder if he's not careful. But he's too busy reading the Daily Bulletin.

I get up, pat my face and neck dry with my towel and head towards the older man, "I'm sorry, sir," I say, "But do I know you?"

It's only right that I approach him with this question, rather than immediately point out that he's making a fool of himself.

He turns to me, "I don't believe so," he says, but he too has a look in his eyes like he's trying to place me.

"We dined at The Restaurant last night, perhaps we saw each other there?" I say.

He shakes his head and laughs. It's an embarrassed laugh, "I doubt it. My wife and I were not seated."

It dawns on me then.

The thick-set lady at the entrance. Her amusing expression of horror as she was told they had to book in advance for a table. This was the man standing beside her. No doubt her husband. *Nouveau riche.*

I extend my hand, "Victor," I tell him, "Victor Peñasco."

He takes it. He has a firm grip, "James Brown," he says.

We smile at each other.

"Say, how about I make reservations tonight for a party of four?"

I don't know why I said it. It just came out. But this man intrigues me. And I'd like to know how he and his wife came to be here, one of the most extraordinary environments in the world.

He nods his head at me once, grateful, "My wife and I would certainly enjoy that."

I smile, *Mine won't.*

"You invited them?" Maria says, looking at me through the reflection in the mirror, "To sit with us?"

She was halfway through applying the bright red lipstick I like so much. The one that makes her mouth look like a ripe strawberry.

I shrug, tossing my towel onto the bed. I walk naked across the room.

"It might be an interesting evening," I say as I pull open the wardrobe and select a white shirt.

Maria opens her mouth to speak when her maid Mina enters the room.

"*Perdona me!*" she yelps as she covers her eyes and turns back around, "I come back later."

I look from Mina's retreating back to my wife sitting at the dressing table. We share a comical chuckle, then she turns back to the mirror, continuing to apply her lipstick.

"You know how important it is to uphold our reputation," she says now as I pull on my underwear and socks, "We shouldn't be seen to mingle with such people."

I sigh noisily, showing her that I am done with the conversation. But she persists.

"They do not have the manners," she complains, "They don't even know to book a dinner table in advance, for goodness sakes!"

I raise an eyebrow, button my shirt.

"What will people think of us when we walk in with them?" She's standing in front of me now, half dressed in her corset and stockings. She looks incredible.

"Do you want people to think less of us?" she asks.

I don't reply. Instead, I take her in as she stands gloriously before me. What I wouldn't do to smudge that perfect lipstick right now.

I reach for her, "You know," I say, "This trip will be a lot more enjoyable if we didn't talk quite so much."

I hook her garter with one finger, pull her closer, then let go of the elastic. It slaps her thigh with a satisfying *snap!* and she yelps under her breath.

I look up at her. She's smiling.

"What about Mina?" she asks quietly as my hands caress her buttocks.

She doesn't care that Mina is in earshot either, because she's already unbuttoning my shirt.

"Let her listen," I say as I pull her on top of me.

And I finally get the thanks I was owed for last night's efforts.

Ethel

We'd spent the morning in bed, but I had insisted we take a walk outside after lunch.

The air was so *clean* here, so crisp and refreshing. I am sure that I have never breathed any air that was cleaner.

It was a beautiful, sunny day, but fresh. After all, it was still only April.

"Look at the colours," I say after a while, walking the public footpath.

Edward follows my gaze, shielding his eyes from the sun with his hand. His face is all screwed up as he looks.

"Incredible, isn't it?" he agrees.

I can hear children laughing as we stroll, our arms locked together. Men are talking in groups, smoking their pipes and cigars, and women are chattering as they pour over the gossip column of the newspaper.

Everyone appears at ease, enjoying their time in the sunshine.

"Perhaps one day we could come back and do this again?" I say now as I turn to look at my handsome new husband, "Maybe we'll return and book a family room."

Edward grins down at me, squeezes my hand in the crook of his arm.

We fall silent again, enjoying each other's company without needing to fill the gaps. It felt wonderful, knowing that we shared the same hopes for our future.

I'd wanted to be a mother for as long as I could remember. Even before Edward had asked for my hand in marriage.

There was never much I was particularly interested in. I enjoyed reading and writing, enjoyed early morning walks, and the mighty silence of nature. But nothing *productive* – as my mother used to complain – ever really captivated me. I guess you could say I was a lover of the simpler things. I was content with the prospects of a modest life. Marry, have children, watch them grow, take care of the household. I was happy with that. More than happy. It was all I hoped for.

A little girl darts across us then, breaking my train of thought, her messy blond hair trailing behind her like a veil.

"Wait for me, William!" she shouts, before disappearing around a corner.

I smile after her. This really was the safest place on Earth to be. And I would most *definitely* want to bring our future children back here.

The equipment cannot be left unattended, so we take our breaks around each other.
It is my turn to get some rest, and I don't waste it.
At the canteen, I eat a hearty meal of lamb stew and bread. I wash it down with a splash of whiskey, then I head straight to my berth and fall into bed.
I have four hours until my next shift, so there's no time to waste on washing. I promise myself I will scrub some of the dirt and sweat off me on my next break, but sleep takes me before I even finish my thou—

Michel

We've been travelling for a while now, so I know the boys are in need of rest, which works well for me because the less time we spend out and about, the better.

Before this part of our trip, we were in London, Dover, Calais, and Paris. A circuitous route to reach our final destination. It would have been simpler to travel directly from Paris, but the whole idea was *not* to have a simple journey.

So far, the boys have been loving this adventure with their papa. But it has been a while since they have seen their mother now, and my youngest, Edmond, is beginning to feel an ache for her. I met their mother some years after I moved from Slovakia, to Hungary, to France in search of a better life. I found it there, in Nice, when I opened my own business.

I was a respected and – dare I say it – successful tailor. Life was good! And things only got better when I married my beautiful wife, Marcelle, just five years later.

Our marriage was a relatively happy one, I would say. On my part, at least, there were no issues. We had our two strapping sons, and the business was doing well.

I still don't know why she chose to throw it all away for an affair…

"Papa?" Edmond's voice snaps me out of my thoughts now. I look up from the picture Master and I are drawing at the desk and plant a smile on my face.

"*Bonjour, mon petit,*" I say, "Are you feeling better?"

He nods his little head.

"Papa, I need blue," Master says beside me, his little hand opening and closing in quick succession, demanding I hand over the crayon.

I allow him to claim it, watch him as he furiously rubs the colour back and forth on the paper.

"It's the beach!" he exclaims proudly.

"I'm hungry," Edmond whines from the top bunk then, and my stomach drops.

I had hoped to remain in our room for at least the rest of the evening and perhaps emerge tomorrow morning.

But I guess we cannot live off the biscuits I packed, alone. My growing boys need nourishment! And what kind of father would I be if I denied them a healthy meal. What kind of example would I be setting?

Certainly no better example than their mother was setting for them when she was spreading her legs for any man who looked at her sideways.

I shake my head free of my upset. That was in the past. And I would leave it there.

"Come on then," I say, standing up to pluck Edmond from the bed, "Let's hunt down some dinner."

At the entrance of the dining room, the concierge looks at me with an expectant smile, "Name?" he says, holding a pencil in his hand.

"Louis Hoffman," I mumble, then clear my throat.

I hold Master and Edmond by the hands, suddenly extremely aware of the presence of my tongue.

I lick my lips as I watch the concierge search the list before him, then tick a little box beside the name I gave.

He looks up at me, his smile brighter than before.

"Please take a seat."

I nod my head and lead my children inside, taking a seat at the far end of the diner.

"I wonder what they have for us today," I say, forcing an excited look upon my face.

Edmond grabs his fork and starts banging it on the table.

"Papa?" Master squeaks, barely audible over Edmond's banging.

"Stop that, Mon," I say to my two-year-old, but he ignores me, bangs it again.

I try to take it.

"No!" he retorts, pulling away and out of my reach.

"Papa?" Master tries again, as Edmond turns in his seat to bang the fork on the back of his chair.

"Mon, turn around!" I hiss at my youngest.

I look over at the other people, some of them with children just as young as mine, none of *them* misbehaving.

A cold sweat begins to seep from my forehead.

Edmond turns around and I seize my opportunity.

"Give me that!" I say to Edmond, snatching the fork from him.

He juts out his bottom lip.

"Papa?"

"What is it, Master?" I say, acknowledging him now that there is some peace.

But then Edmond opens his mouth and lets out a loud wail, his eyes squeezing out big, fat tears from the corners of his eyes.

People are looking at us. It is the last thing I want…

The two tables closest to us are watching me, judging, based on the thirty seconds they've known me.

"It's okay, Mon," I say, my hands fluttering over him, wiping his face with my palms, "Here, why don't you read the menu for me? Huh? Here," I press the menu into his chubby hands, "Look, what should papa eat?"

He sniffles, looks down at the letters, none of them making sense to him.

Then he looks up at me, his cheeks red from crying but a small smile tugging on his lips.

"Chicken poop and grass!" he offers then, his outburst forgotten as quickly as it had begun. I gift him a chuckle, glad to have been able to distract him.

I turn to Master, finally able to give him my full attention, "What is it, son?"

"Why did you tell that man your name is Louis Hoffman?"

Catherine

William and I are finally allowed outside thanks to Miss Alice offering to watch us.

Miss Alice is a friend of the family, I have known her all my life, and it is because of her that my parents decided on this adventure.

Alice's cousin had recommended it. Or maybe it was a friend of hers? I'm not sure.

We *were* supposed to do this back in October last year, but Mother and Father decided to postpone it, so that Alice could come with us.

And I sure am glad that we waited.

It's my turn to play with the spinning top, so I hold out my hand to William. He hands it over reluctantly, knowing that to mess around and argue about it would only get us sent back to our room.

I spin it as hard as I can, and William and I watch it as it turns round and round.

It's peaceful up here. There's loadsa people walking up and down, loads more sitting around sipping drinks or reading a book on the loungers. But everyone's happy. There are no raised voices, no shouting across to each other. Not like inside. Out here I can hear the sound of the waves at every turn. It's very calming.

"My turn, Cat," William says then, interrupting my peace as he snatches the string from my hand.

"Hey!" I shout at him.

"What?" he retorts, "You gonna tell *mummy?*"

He says it mockingly, because I have only recently stopped calling our mother that. William had made me, really. Had said it was what babies called their mothers. I had tried to ignore him, but big brothers being big brothers, he teased me until I gave in.

She is 'Mother' now. Has been for the last six months.

So, I don't know why he's saying it now, as if I still call her it! I don't!

"I'm not a baby!" I say, stomping my foot.

"Children," Miss Alice's voice calls lazily from where she's sitting. She doesn't even look up from her book, she's so used to our fighting.

I make a face at William and walk over to Alice, plonking down beside her, my arms crossed as I sulk.

"What are you reading?" I ask her after a moment.

"The Secret Garden by Frances Hodgson Burnett," she tells me without looking up.

I glance over at it, "Is it good?"

Alice looks up at me then, her hand, which had been absentmindedly picking at her lower lip, falls into her lap.

"Yes," she tells me simply.

She frowns at me then, "You might like it actually," she says, before handing it to me, "Here, take it."

"But you're reading it!" I argue.

She shrugs, "I've read it before."

I look at the cover. A young blond girl dressed in a red frock is trying to unlock a hidden door in a hedge.

"What's it about?" I ask.

Miss Alice grins at me, tucks a lock of my unruly hair behind my ear, "It's about a secret garden, of course."

Victor

Brown and his wife are loud, raucous. And I know that it's making my wife cringe.

The wife was telling a story, interrupting herself throughout as she laughed at her own tale. It wasn't particularly funny, but the champagne had been flowing during dinner and the mood was catching, so I laughed along with her and her husband.

At the end of her humorous narrative, she picks up her napkin and dabs at the corners of her eyes.

"Do make an effort, my dear," I tell Maria in Spanish now as I lean into her, obscuring my command with a toothy smile. I reach underneath the tablecloth and subtly grab her thigh for good measure.

"Tell me, Mrs Brown –"

"Margaret, please!" the wife interrupts Maria, "I've told you. Call me Margaret."

Maria forces a smile, "Margaret. Do tell me: How did you and your husband come about your fortune?"

I choke on my champagne, nearly dropping the crystal glass onto my plate of lamb, "*Maria!*" I exclaim, embarrassed.

But Margaret laughs, waves her chunky hand in the air, "Oh no, we don't mind discussing our stroke of luck, do we darling?"

He shakes his head as he cuts into his chateau potatoes. I frown at his response. Talk of business is not suitable amongst women!

"James' mining engineering efforts proved instrumental back in the 90's, in the exploration of a substantial ore seam," Margaret was telling Maria. My wife was nodding along, as if any of the woman's jabber meant anything to her, "He is one of the major owners of the Ibex Mining Company, and has mining enterprises in Leadville, Arizona, the Southwest –"

"That's enough Maggie," Brown's voice cut in then, and I exhale with relief.

I'm surprised he allowed her to go on as much as she did. But I'm more disgruntled by my own wife's lack of decorum. One did not ask about another's fortune at *dinner!*

But one thing was for sure, at least. Maria had been right: they were indeed new money.

We fall silent then, the only sound being that of our cutlery against porcelain and the elegant music of the orchestra seeping in from the lounge.

But the quiet did not last long, the wife inhaling deeply to share a new story with no doubt as much gusto as the previous one.

I grin at her as she speaks uninhibitedly, half in anticipation of the punchline, half in thanks for brushing the awkward moment aside.

I was enjoying their company. But as I glance at Maria beside me, I know I won't ask them to dinner again. Not when Maria feels so uncomfortable.

After all, we were still on our honeymoon. And what kind of husband would I be if I forced such obvious discomfort onto my wife?

DAY THREE

Ethel

I'd never had a boyfriend before Edward.

Becoming engaged at fourteen will see to that, I guess.

But I often wondered over the six years that I waited for Edward to return to me, if perhaps it would've been a good idea to sneak a kiss from another boy. Just to get a little experience. After all, my future husband was thirteen years my senior, with his own past encounters.

But I never did, not even when Tommy Lloyd wrote me that love letter. Not even when he confessed one Sunday morning that he'd had dreams of us holding hands. Not even when he had reached up and tucked a strand of my hair behind my ear.

I'd liked Tommy. He and I had grown up together.

But he did not hold a candle to my Edward.

Anyway, I hear he's engaged to Lydia Thomson from down the road now, so I guess we're all where we are meant to be.

"Tea, darling?" Edward asks me now over breakfast.

I respond with a smile and watch as he pours the hot, amber liquid into the pretty floral cup.

"What should we do today?" I ask him once he sets down the teapot.

He inhales deeply as he thinks, pops a piece of buckwheat cake into his mouth. His moustache moves up and down, as if it has a heartbeat of its own. I smile secretly at my thoughts.

"How about a game of quoits?" he finally suggests.

I lean in to peck him on the cheek, "Wonderful idea, husband."

*

The weather continues bright and tranquil, the perfect atmosphere for an outing.

And it seems we weren't the only ones with this idea, many surrounding us with their own quoits rings, or lounging in the sunshine with a book.

"I may need some assistance," I tell Edward now as I plant my feet firmly in position, "I am not the most graceful of quoits players."

Edward chuckles but does not move from his spot beside me. He puffs on his pipe, observing my hands.

"Well, alright," I say under my breath before tossing the ring. It lands nowhere near my intended goal.

Edward erupts in laughter, "My dear!" he says, his pipe dangling from the side of his mouth.

"I told you," I laugh.

"Here," he says as he approaches me now. He stands behind me, pressing his chest against my back as he takes my hands in his and gently demonstrates how best to hit the mark.

"Keep the wrist loose," he says, his voice sounding tender and warm in my ear, like a splash of brandy, "Then flick it just so," and together we throw the ring.

It lands beside the peg, but much closer than its companion, which lay a good two feet away.

"Much better," Edward says as he continues to hold me from behind, his big hands clutching my arms.

I look over my shoulder and into his smiling brown eyes, then step aside to allow him his turn.

The sound of happy laughter and screeching makes us both turn around.

A little boy, no older than perhaps four or five, is chasing after a smaller version of himself, both of them beaming brightly at the pursuit. The little one at the front – who was probably about three? – kept looking over his shoulder to ascertain his distance from his pursuer, his cheeks flushed pink from the excitement. But then the little one loses his footing and falls right before my eyes, and his previous giggling is replaced with a piercing shriek.

At the sound, many look up from their games and their books. But because I'd been watching the children, my reaction comes quicker, and before any of the other onlookers has the time to react, I've already picked up my skirts and hurry towards them.

I crouch down and scoop the little one up as the older boy breathes shakily before me.

I gently *shush* the boy in my arms, turn to who I assume is his brother, "What's his name?" I calmly ask him.

The older boy only blinks at me, "*Mon papa est là-bas. Il m'a dit de ne pas aller trop loin...*"

With the little one screaming into my right ear and the older one speaking in a language I don't understand, I begin to feel flustered.

I stand up and look back at Edward, who was now standing beside me.

"Do you speak French?" I ask him.

It feels like the strangest thing to ask the man I have just married. Isn't that something I should already know?

Edward shakes his head at me, and I feel oddly relieved.

The cries of the boy in my arms have reduced to mere hiccups by now, and I turn a smiling face to him.

"There," I say as I wipe the tears from his cheeks with the back of my hand.

I feel a tug at my dress, and I look down to see the older boy pointing along the boulevard.

"*Mon papa arrive,*" he says.

I look up to where he is pointing and see a tall, slim-built man stalking towards us.

I feel a little uneasy at the sight of him suddenly, though I don't know why.

"*Master, Edmond, Je t'ai dit de rester proche,*" he says in their language as he scoops the little boy out of my arms.

"He fell," I tell him, as though to defend my reason for picking up his child.

The man looks from his little boy, to me.

"Thank you," he says in English, and I relax somewhat.

"I said they could play but not to go too far," he explains, his accent prominent.

I smile at him reassuringly, then look to Edward.

The man extends his free hand to me then, "Louis Hoffman," he says as I shake his hand, "And this is John and Fred."

The older boy, standing before his father now, looks up at him, and Mr Hoffman places a hand on his blond head, pats it tenderly.

"Nice to meet you," I say with a genuine smile, glad to see little Fred has stopped crying, "I am Ethel, and this is my husband, Edward."

The men shake hands, nod at each other in greeting.

"Well," Mr Hoffman says after a beat of awkward silence, "Thanks again."

He turns away, one son held in his arm, the other by the hand. I watch them go, more sure than ever that I am ready to be a mother, the warm feeling of longing taking over my entire body.

I turn to Edward to tell him how the encounter made me feel, when I notice the frown between his brows.

I take his arm, and we walk back to our game.

"What is it, Edward?" I ask.

He shakes his head briefly, his mouth downturned as he thinks, "Probably nothing."

I look back at the retreating man and his young sons, "Do you know him?"

He turns to me, a smile on his lips, "Oh no," and he bends over to pick up the metal rings.

"What then?" I prompt.

He shrugs lightly, "I probably misheard. But I was sure he had called his sons 'Master' and 'Edmond.'"

Thomas

I don't much care to listen to talk, preferring to simply keep my head down and get my work done.

But when I heard the same report being whispered among the men again and again, I have to assume it's serious.

The fire from the other day has been put out, but it appears it was but the first of many minor issues we would be facing.

"We've had at least four warnings so far," my colleague was telling me as we continued to work.

"*Four?*" I repeat then, frankly shocked. I step away from my work, "Should we lay off?"

He shakes his head, "Bell says no."

I inhale deeply, raise my eyebrows.

But it wasn't our job to ask questions. Our job was to keep things going.

So, I drop my head back down and continue to do just that.

I knew I shouldn't have allowed myself to get distracted, but when I was asked by a fellow Frenchman to play a game of cards, I couldn't say no.

I'd been so on edge lately, our trip proving a lot more challenging than I'd thought, and I hadn't realised how much I'd needed some time to relax.

But not again. I could not take my eyes off the ball, not when we were so close to our destination. Just a couple more days of rest and we would be on our way.

"Who's Fred?" Edmond asks me now as I descend the few steps from the games area.

I half look over my shoulder to gauge the distance between us and the young couple we just met. Satisfied we were far enough away that they did not hear Edmond's question to me, I leave it unanswered.

I lead the boys back inside, Master trailing behind me as fast as his little legs can carry him.

I slow down once we have made our way to our hallway, put Edmond down. He can safely walk the rest of the way from here.

"Papa, papa!" he calls now as he toddles quickly ahead of me. He throws a look over his shoulder, grinning that adorable grin of his.

I flash him a smile and Master zooms past me to try to catch his bud. Edmond squeals as he realises his brother's hot pursuit and I allow the moment to fill my heart.

This is where my focus should be. Not on a card game with some stranger.

I'm disappointed in myself. And I begin to wonder if I am doing the right thing…

Once in our room, I set the boys up with their crayons and fresh sheets of paper to draw on, before taking a seat on the uncomfortable sofa to write a letter.

I address it to my mother in Hungary, though in its contents I ask if my sister and her husband would look after my sons.

I look up at them after a moment of writing. They are sitting so nicely together, each drawing on their own respective sheets of paper. Master's tongue is sticking out the side of his mouth, as it often did when he was completely focused on something. At least, I *think* that's what he often does.

A sad smile creeps over my lips, and I duck my head back down to finish the letter.

I don't want my boys to live with my sister. Not really.

But I need a safety net, a backup plan, in case this one was to go awry.

"Look, Master!" Edmond's voice calls then, breaking our companionable silence.

I look up to see what Edmond wants Master to look at. He's proudly holding up his picture.

Master lifts his gaze briefly, nods unimpressed.

Edmond scrunches up his face, and I know a tantrum is to follow, so I quickly ask him to show it to me, hoping to spare his feelings, and my eardrums.

He turns the paper to me, and I gasp animatedly at the red and yellow squiggles he's produced on the page.

"*Fantastique!*" I announce, clapping my hands together.

Edmond grins at me – I have succeeded in saving his good mood.

"Can we send it to mama?" he asks me then as he picks up the orange crayon, and a lump forms in my throat.

"But of course, my boy," I tell him, returning to my letter. Though I have absolutely no intention of doing anything of the sort.

Victor

I stretch out my neck, my eyes cast skyward, as the barber, Augustus Weikman, runs the sharp razor along my jawline.

He does not speak to me, hardly speaks to any of his customers from what I can tell.

But his silence was what I enjoyed most about him. A chit-chatting barber was not for me. I never understood the appeal. What am I to say to a man as he holds a sharp blade at my throat? Surely to laugh at a silly joke or to reply to an inane question could lead to getting your jugular sliced!

No, thank you.

But when I spot *him* strolling into the barber shop from the corner of my eye, I cannot help but turn in my seat.

I hear Weikman grunt in displeasure at my sudden movement, but I don't feel a nick to my skin – thank heavens – and I'm able to dismiss my error in judgement without apology.

"John!" I exclaim, as though we are old friends, "Here to have your moustache trimmed?"

I grin at him, turning up my charm.

He eyeballs me suspiciously for a moment, but I maintain my leer and I can tell that he is trying to figure out if he knows me from somewhere.

Admitting defeat, his face crumples into a friendly smile, "The wife prefers a smooth chin," he admits.

He runs a hand over it to emphasise his point.

"Ah, yes," I say, then, "Wives," with a scoff.

I raise an eyebrow at him, and he offers me a chuckle.

And *that's* how easy it is to establish common ground with a stranger in our circle.

"How is your new wife, my good man?" I say now as I turn back around to face the disgruntled barber.

John does not know me. Not really. He may have heard of me by name – but since I have not yet given it to him, and he is too polite to ask – he continues with the charade that we are at least acquaintances.

"She is well," he says, keeping the information brisk. Then, "And yours?"

I wonder if he's seen me and Maria at dinner or in the lounge, or if he is taking a wild stab in the dark that I am married. Though, most men my age would be married. Unless there was something wrong with them…

I smile at his risk, reward him for being right, "Maria is very well," I offer, "She and I are on the last leg of our honeymoon."

"Indeed?" he says, as if he cares.

I nod as the barber steps away to survey his work, then wipes my face and throat with a white towel.

I turn around in the chair, face the moustached man.

"Perhaps you would like to join my wife and I for dinner tomorrow?" I say with a smirk, dismissing the little voice in my head that reminds me that Maria would not approve.

And besmirch our reputation?

But John shakes his head, "Perhaps another time," he says as he takes a seat beside me and Weikman throws the white cape over him, securing it around his neck.

"My wife and I are entertaining tomorrow," he says, offering his excuse.

I must admit, I feel snubbed.

But I don't show it. Instead, I flash him my brightest smile and rise from my seat.

"Next time, then," I say, a hint of demand to my tone.
The older man turns to me, nods once, "Next time."

Maria is none the wiser that I conversed with John, much less that I invited him and his 'little wife' to dinner.
So, when he nods his head at us in greeting at the entrance to The Restaurant, Maria looks to me with one of her thinly-plucked eyebrows raised high.
"Making friends wherever you go, Victor," she says in jest.
I don't tell her that her joke is actually completely accurate, and that by the time this trip is over, I plan to have, at least, gained some rapport with one of the richest men in the world. Because scandal or not… well, he was one of the richest men in the world…
After dinner, we retreat to the lounge, where the band – an octet orchestra including three violinists, three cellists, a bassist, and a pianist – were playing a waltz.
With a belly full of filet mignon, a cigar lit and a Cognac in my hand, I felt as relaxed as could be, considering we were in the middle of nowhere.
I close my eyes and allow the feeling to consume my entire body.
"I thought that was you!"
The obnoxiously loud voice interrupts my peace, and I know, even before I open my eyes, who it belongs to.
"Mrs Brown," I say politely, plastering on a smile.
"Margaret, please!" she laughs, before taking a seat on one of the armchairs near us.
Maria and I exchange a quick glance, and I can immediately tell that we are on the same wavelength.

Personally, I had nothing against the woman, though I couldn't say the same for Maria. But right now, I did not care for raucous conversation.

"We were just headed back," I tell her as I bring my glass to my lips and down the Cognac in one.

The warm liquid both soothes and burns my throat, but I don't let the discomfort show.

"Oh?" Margaret says.

If she can see through my lie, she doesn't intimate it. New money or not, at least she had some class.

"James will be sorry he missed you," she says instead, as she raises a hand in the air and looks over my shoulder with an open-mouthed smile.

I don't follow her gaze.

"We should get going," I say, standing up and offering Maria my arm.

"So good to see you, Mrs Brown."

Maria drops the statement into the older woman's lap like a bag of vipers, the formal use of her name despite the numerous requests to call her 'Margaret', a clear sign that a friendship would not blossom here.

I shake my head at Maria slightly as we walk away.

"I had it handled," I told her under my breath once we escaped the lounge and made our way through the lobby and towards the wide, curved staircase to our room.

Maria doesn't reply.

I turn to look at her, but she ignores me, her own, perfectly made-up eyes downcast as she walks. There's a tiny smirk twitching at the corners of her mouth though, so I know the night isn't over yet.

I allow my gaze to roll down her neck and along her shoulder, which is bare this evening on account of her new dress, a navy blue off-the-shoulder garb designed by one of today's most respectable designers.

I imagine the dress crumpled in a blue heap at the foot of the bed in our suite, a puddle of fabric, its wearer naked and vulnerable in my arms –

"Isn't that your tailor?"

Maria's question shatters the wonderful image in my head, and I turn an irritated gaze up to where she is looking.

I have a handful of tailors I like to frequent, all over Europe. So I don't know which one she means. But when I spot the man among the crowd, I frown.

"It is," I say, slightly stunned to see him here.

"Those must be his sons," Maria adds absentmindedly, her interest already slipping.

I grunt in agreement. Then I raise my chin, "Mr Navratil!"

The man stops in his tracks, and, strangely, he appears rather spooked. At the sound of his name, his back goes stiff and his face pales, and I am sure I see his hands tightening their grip on his young sons'.

"Mr Navratil, I thought I recognised you," I say as Maria and I approach, "Well, Maria, here, recognised you. What a coincidence to see you here, Michel."

Michel offers me a forced smile, "Mr Peñasco, sir, it's good to see you."

He doesn't mean it. In fact, I'm pretty sure he means the complete opposite.

I wonder what he's hiding. Probably an affair.

"What brings you here?" I ask, hoping to gain some knowledge into what scandal is no doubt brewing.

"Business," Michel Navratil answers much too quickly.

"Business?" I parrot.

He doesn't reply. Doesn't break eye contact either. I admire that.

A smirk escapes me, "How is the wife?"

Michel looks uncomfortably down at the little lads on either side of him then, bookending him like two porcelain dolls.

He clears his throat and leans forward, so much so that I can smell his desperation.

"She is dead, sir," he mutters under his breath so that the boys will not hear.

At the announcement, I must admit I feel flustered.

"Oh," I mumble, taken aback, "My apologies, my good man, I did not know."

Michel shakes his head, his eyes dramatically wide as he carefully jerks his chin down to indicate his sons.

It's my turn to clear my throat, "Yes, yes," I say, trying to regain my composure.

To my amazement, Maria reaches over and squeezes his arm, "You're a good father," she tells him, a shine in her eyes.

Navratil looks uncomfortable, and I'm not sure if it's at the compliment, at my wife's touch…or something else.

Ethel

We are in the lounge room of our floor, where people tend to gather for the evening.

It is after dinner; Edward and I having enjoyed a splendid spread of baked haddock and roast turkey.

Our bellies are full, and we are satisfied beyond measure.

After aiding little Fred from his fall and meeting the boys' father, Edward was a little out of sorts. He got himself worked up, wondering what reasons the man could have had to lie to two perfect strangers.

I didn't like to see Edward so unnerved, and in the interest of returning his mind to our honeymoon, I suggested some afternoon delight.

To my amazement, all it had taken was a gentle hand on his chest, one suggestively raised eyebrow, and in an instant, Edward had grabbed me by the hand – our quoits game forgotten – and eagerly led me back inside and to our room. We spent the day there, skipping lunch. Only coming up for air when we could no longer breathe in the stiflingly small room, its oxygen having been spent.

But now, as we sit side by side on one of the love seats in the general room, I take a moment to cast my eye over my fellow lodgers.

In the far corner, a man plays on the piano, a cheery but gentle tune filling the air, a welcome undertone to the buzz of conversation coming from the people at the tables.

Almost every seat is taken tonight, the adults chatting and laughing while the many children run around, making friends with anyone at that age.

I smile as I watch a group of them giggling, sitting cross legged in a circle. One of them, a girl, is telling a story, gesticulating wildly with her hands while the others listen, occasionally asking questions. There are boys and girls in this group. They appear to be of a range of ages, the youngest appearing around five, the eldest maybe twelve?

I wonder if they knew each other before this.

Across the room, a pair of lovers sit closely together at the bar, whispering to one another as they sit so near, they may as well be kissing. He's rubbing her bare forearm with the tips of his fingers, and a shiver runs over me as a memory of this afternoon flashes in my mind.

I smile at Edward beside me, though he doesn't notice, and shuffle closer to him.

The room is *packed*, the dining room, too, had been almost full! This establishment was so vast!

And yet somehow, I keep seeing the same people.

"Isn't that Mr Hoffman and his sons?" I ask Edward as I nudge my chin straight ahead.

He follows my gaze, squints through the smoke of his pipe, "Oh, yes."

I nod slowly, "Should we ask them to join us?"

Edward looks at me sideways, blows smoke out the side of his mouth, "No."

The directness of his answer surprises me.

"Why not?" I ask, continuing to watch the father and son trio snaking their way through the many people and tables.

Edward cautiously points his pipe at them, "That man is hiding something," he says matter-of-factly.

I breathe a laugh, "Oh, Edward. You may have misheard."
Edward nods, but his eyebrows are raised, "Perhaps. But I know a shifty fellow when I see one."
My eyes are wide as he says this, and I tear my stare from my husband to observe Mr Hoffman again, this time through a different lens.

"Do you think the children are unsafe?" I don't know why I ask this. It was the first thought that popped in my head, my womanly instinct kicking in, wanting to protect the little ones.
But Edward scoffs, "Of course not!" he says, and I feel a little foolish, "I don't believe the man to be a *murderer*, intent on hurting his own. He could've stayed at home to do that!"
He pops his pipe back in his mouth, talks around it, "No. I mean only that he is not here for the luxuries, my dear. *That* man is here in hiding."

<u>*Thomas*</u>

I remember taking William and Thomas to Belfast last year, to show them what their old man had been working on for so many years.

William was only four at the time, so I'm not sure how much he understood of my excited ramblings about my work. But Thomas was in awe. I could tell.

I'd felt proud that day. Proud of all my hard work, sleepless nights, days away from home, coming to fruition.

I won't deny that I'm an ambitious man: I've always wanted to make something of myself.

But I'd lost some of that fire when Jennie was diagnosed, as I'm sure is only natural.

I hid myself away during that period, spent a lot of time at home, my work neglected. And ironically, I was *finally* where I should have been all along. But too late.

I was mostly at Jennie's side in those final weeks, our sons spending many nights at their Aunt Matilda's. And when Jennie slipped away, I practically disappeared in on myself. The grief was so intense. It was unlike anything I'd ever felt.

Suddenly my work no longer mattered. *I* no longer mattered. I felt like there was no achievement I could ever pursue that would equate to that of being Jennie's husband. And I regret to say it, but not even being a father.

It took some time to get out of my fog. In fact, I'm not even sure I have found my way out of it quite yet.

But then this position was offered to me, the prestigious honour to work within the very enterprise I had helped to create.

Originally, I had been unsure about it – unsure about leaving my sons so soon after their mother's death. But I was so rarely there in these last few months, what was a few more days if it meant their father would return to them perhaps a little healed? And if not a little healed, then at least with a few more bob lining our pockets.

Now that I am here, I am quickly realising that *this* – hard work – was exactly what I'd needed all along. And I am glad now that I accepted the opportunity.

As I stop to wipe the sweat from my brow with my forearm, I think back on that cold Sunday morning of 1911, when I'd brought my boys to show them my work – back before Jennie had died, back before our world had crumbled.

My sons' slack-jawed faces of wonder as they stared up at the grand construction will stay with me forever.

Thomas had turned to me, impressed, and my chest had filled with accomplishment. I recall thinking in that moment that even if I wasn't remembered by the world, my sons, at least, would make me feel like I'd achieved something great with my life. Something worth talking about. And it was enough that I'd made *them* proud at least.

"Titanic," Thomas had breathed, reading the name off the large ship's side.

I'd nodded at him, then bent down to pick William up and into my arms. We all craned our necks to look up at the magnificent vessel together.

"Aye," I'd said with a delighted grin, "Titanic."

DAY FOUR

Michel

When I moved to Nice in search of a better life and began my tailor and dressmaking business, I never believed for a moment that I would be so lucky as to gain customers such as Victor Peñasco.

I did not know who he was when he first waltzed into my shop that first day, but I immediately knew from the cut of his suit and the angle of his chin that he was of money.

Old money.

To my credit, I didn't gush over his presence or brown-nose up to him because of his obvious fortune. No doubt he received that kind of treatment everywhere he went already.

Instead, I approached him as I would any client, with my charm dialled up just enough to show respect but not so much that it degraded my own self-worth.

I would not let him know how desperately I needed his – or anyone's – custom.

Maybe he admired my ability to withhold my elation, or maybe he just really liked my fine work on his suit. Whatever it was, Victor Peñasco would return every couple of months, whenever his leisurely life brought him back to Nice.

Over the years, he was not the only regular upper-class client that I had of course, but he now remained one of the few who, because of his sporadic use of my services, did not yet know that my small company had gone bust.

I count my small fortunes for that now. Because our encounter on the Titanic could have been that much more awkward. For one, he would have known immediately that my reason for being on this ship – *business* – had been a blatant lie.

I was not here on business. Unless you count relocating and beginning anew in New York as such.

Come to think of it, I guess in some ways it is…

It's a much nicer way to look at things, actually. Much more pleasant than 'running from the law', 'hiding from authorities', 'fleeing from justice'.

But no, the real reason as to why we are here, on this luxury passenger ship on its maiden voyage across the Atlantic, was because no one would *expect* us to be.

Years ago, my wife Marcelle had meant everything to me. She, our sons, and my business had been my entire world.

She was originally from Italy, I from Slovakia, and we always found it so strangely beautiful that we would find each other while we were both so far away from home.

It hadn't *felt* like a whirlwind romance. It had felt like we'd known each other for years.

And when she agreed to come to Nice with me, I believed it only right that we do so as man and wife. And so, on the 26th of May 1907, just two months after our first meeting, we were wed. In London. Because it was the only place that would allow it.

It was one of the best days of my life.

Master was born shortly thereafter – another day to add to my bests – and then Edmond – another.

We were happy.

But then her eyes wandered…and our perfect life was ruined.

It was my fault. At least in part. I knew I was spending too much time at the shop. But what was I to do when it was haemorrhaging more money than it was bringing in?

She told me his name was *Edward*. Such a stiflingly dull name.

But she proclaimed that he made her 'happy', that he would 'care for her, and our sons'.

Yes, our sons.

Our, I'd reminded her. Not *his*.

But I'd agreed to let her take them. My two boys. At least until I'd figured everything out.

I let her take them. And I promised them I would make it right. Which was exactly what I am doing.

Catherine

Miss Alice and I are hunched over her copy of The Secret Garden, both of us reading it in tandem in the Open Room. Well, actually Miss Alice is going back and forth between reading with me and drawing, but I appreciate the company all the same.

William left me alone this morning, when our parents allowed us to go play. I knew where he was, of course, he was only over there, across the room.

But he specifically told me to stay away. To leave him alone, while he went to sit with a pretty brunette girl and her friends, around his age.

Carefully lifting my gaze from the pages before me, I look after him now. He's just a few yards away, but he may as well be back on dry land, he's pretending so hard that I don't exist. Boys are so weird. And so are those girls for that matter!

They are only two years older than me, and yet they're giggling at William's stupid jokes as if they were actually funny. The brunette one is…twirling her hair around her finger…

I shake my head, my face screwed up in mild disgust. I'll never understand it. Nine-year-olds are so peculiar.

I return to my book.

In the story, Mary, the girl in the red frock on the cover, has just begun tending to the secret garden, and I'm glad to find that it's helping her overcome her grief after losing her parents and moving to England after a lifetime in India.

I can't even imagine that kind of tragedy. It must be devastating to lose your parents. I'm sure I'd die of grief if I ever lost mine.

I look over to Alice, who has returned to her drawing. She's shading in parts of it with her pinkie finger, and I lean closer to see what she's captured.

"What is it?" I ask, trying to place the tables and chairs. Alice looks up briefly, but not at me, directly in front of her. I follow her gaze, then look back at the picture. She's drawn the Open Room, its large empty centre outlined by a few tables and chairs. She's even drawn the bar at the end and the drinking fountain.

"I wish I could draw like that," I mumble, returning back to my book.

Alice shrugs, "You're only seven, Cat," she says, continuing to carefully pencil in the finer details, "When you're a grown up like me, I'm sure you'll have all kinds of special talents."

"I'm not sure I'd like to be a grown up anyway," I mumble, risking a glimpse at William as he and those silly girls laugh at something.

Alice puts her pencil down, finally looking at me.

I meet her eyes, shrug.

"It seems rather dull," I explain.

At that, Miss Alice smiles, a slow stretch of her thin lips as my remark sinks in.

Then she sighs and picks up her pencil once again, "I suppose you're right, Cat," she mutters down at her drawing, "Perhaps we would all do better never to grow up."

Victor

After a quick dip in the heated indoor pool this morning, Maria and I decide to take a leisurely stroll on the boat deck, to soak up the Spring sun.

But we weren't prepared for the cold breeze that would hit us, and within minutes, I was already peeling off my jacket and covering Maria's shoulders.

"Mina, head back to our suite and fetch my fur shawl," Maria orders her maid, who had been trailing behind.

The older woman nods and disappears on her mission.

We begin walking again, slower still, so that Mina can easily find us upon her return, and I wrap my arm around Maria in the meantime, looking up to observe the four great funnels of the Titanic, three of which are puffing out thick clouds of steam.

"It is *not* a 'gargantuan waste of space', Colonel!"

My ears prick up at the loud voice and who it was addressing, and sure enough, a few steps ahead of us is Mrs Brown and her husband, shmoozing with none other than the very man I've been trying to get close to.

Colonel John Jacob Astor.

"Good morning, James!" I call as casually as I can, a broad grin plastered on my face. I just hope Margaret will forgive us our swift exit last night.

They all turn around in unison, as if pulled by the same string. I survey their faces quickly, relieved to see Margaret Brown beaming brightly.

"Mr and Mrs Peñasco!" Mrs Brown says in greeting.

It is my turn to beg for informalities, "Victor, please," I say, and I think I see a small smirk twitching at Mrs Brown's lips.
We probably deserve that hint of contempt.

"What brings you here this fine morning?" Margaret asks, before bursting out a short laugh.

"The sun initially," I say, matching her mood, "But this wind has a sharp chill to it!"

"Indeed," John Astor agrees, and I throw him a grateful smile. There's a beat of awkward silence, but thankfully Mina arrives just then, carrying Maria's fur.
My wife peels off my jacket and I take it from her, glad for the extra layer.

"I was just saying to the Colonel here, that the number of lifeboats on board is appalling!" Margaret says as Maria and I adjust our warmer clothing.

"Appalling?" I repeat, my eyebrows furrowing. I look to John Astor.
The richer man chuckles, "I was telling Mr and Mrs Brown –"

"James and Margaret, please!" Margaret interrupts, and Maria and I share a secret smile.
The Colonel clears his throat, then turns to continue walking. We all follow suit.

"I was telling James and Margaret," he corrects, "that to have lifeboats at all on this ship is a gargantuan waste of space."

"'A waste of space…'" Margaret mutters under her breath, shaking her head, the feather on her wide brim hat flapping in the wind.
I see my opportunity, and I take it, "I must say I agree with the Colonel."
Astor raises an eyebrow at Margaret, as if to say, *See?*

"The Titanic is unsinkable," a short laugh bursts from me, "Everybody knows that!"

"Yes, yes," Margaret says, waving her hand in the air, "But *in case* the lifeboats were to be needed. For whatever reason. There are not enough. Eighteen lifeboats is not enough for the two thousand passengers onboard."

"Two-thousand-two-hundred, I believe," Maria adds casually.

A silence envelops us as we all think about it. But no, it was a moot point. Because we would never come to find out.

"Wasn't there meant to be a drill this morning?" James Brown says then, breaking our silence.

"A drill?" his wife replies.

James nods, "Yes, I heard the captain cancelled it."

"Whatever for?" Margaret asks, "Surely a drill is rather important!"

The Colonel chuckles. And to my horror, Margaret Brown rounds on him.

"It is not a laughing matter, Colonel!"

"Maggie," James rumbles, tampering his wife's outburst like a lid over a pot of bubbling water, "Enough."

"I did not mean to offend," John Astor says, holding up a hand, "But perhaps you will find some comfort in the fact that, surely if the captain himself concludes the drill an unnecessary procedure, then the lifeboats really *are* needless."

"So, your conclusion is simply that I am wrong?" Margaret counters.

I raise my eyebrows at Maria, then subconsciously drop my gaze to her lips as they curve into a slight smirk, and I'm grateful to have a wife who does not dare to talk back.

I suddenly cannot wait to be alone with her.

Colonel John Jacob Astor exhales slowly as he considers his reply, the four of us continuing to walk along the wooden boulevard, Mina trailing behind.

"Yes," he concludes, "I believe that is what I am saying."

<u>*Ethel*</u>

   From the corner of my eye, I see a flash of red blurring past me, and my head whips round almost involuntarily to follow it. I spot the girl I saw on the promenade the other day.

William, wait for me!

Her voice echoes in my mind now.

She's skipping along with who I assume to be her family, one of her hands clasped tightly in her father's, while the other holds a book against her chest.

The Secret Garden.

She sees me looking and I quickly smile to reassure her.

She smiles back at me. She seems very sweet. The young girl and her family disappear through a door that leads downstairs, and I briefly wonder what it's like in third class.

Edward and I are enjoying tea on the spacious outdoor promenade this morning, along with dozens of our fellow second-class passengers.

We are sat in comfortable silence: he, perfectly content reading about the racing in the Daily Bulletin, and I, just as satisfied to people-watch.

There is a group of older women gossiping at one table, while a table beside them hosts a group of men – likely the women's husbands – all of them smoking their pipes or reading the newspaper in total silence. I chuckle at the contrast of the two tables.

Some children are running up and down the length of the promenade, while some others sit cross-legged on the wooden decking, playing cards or dice. I watch two little ginger girls as

they sing a song and play pat-a-cake. As the song goes on, their clapping gains some speed, and I watch in awe before one of them messes up and they both erupt in laughter.
I laugh along with them under my breath.
And above all our noise, the talking, laughing, smoking, and playing, the sound of the ship slicing through the water is very much present. We must be travelling at quite some speed!
"When do we make port, Edward?" I ask my husband then, aware that it should be any day now.
His eyes do not tear from what he is reading, "Should be any day now."
I nod, though it's no more than I already knew.
Edward sighs noisily then and folds the newspaper in half, "It's a little chilly, Ethel," he says as he moves his pipe from one corner of his mouth to the other, "I should like to return indoors."
"Of course," I say as I rise from my seat, "Perhaps we might peruse the library. I believe there will be music around this time?"
He looks at his wristwatch, one that he recently told me was formerly his father's, passed down upon his death some years ago.
Edward grunts in agreement, removes his pipe and pockets it, "We may catch the morning performance if we hurry."
We enter the ship and feel immediately warmer. It may be a sunny day, but the breeze was much colder than it was yesterday, and I have a feeling we won't be braving the outdoors again today.
The library was located on the C-deck at the rear of the ship, and as we approach it, I am glad to hear the string quintet is still playing. It will be so nice to read a good book with the gentle lull in the background.

I nod my head at the musicians in the corner, thanking them for their service with a smile as we walk past.

Edward does not acknowledge them, but I felt it was only right. The library is largely empty, a handful of lone people sitting at their respective desks as they write a letter or mull over the Daily Bulletin.

We select a spot in the corner, both of us with the same idea that we will likely remain here for some time, perhaps even until they served afternoon tea.

After a moment scanning the large bookcase along the far wall, I settle down on the dark green leather seat and make myself comfortable, Edward doing the same on the chair beside me.

We do not say a word to the other, satisfied with a gentle smile before we both dive into our books for the afternoon, oblivious to the world outside, and I briefly wonder *why* it was so chilly out there.

Thomas

As an assistant deck engineer on the Titanic, I was always busy. I, along with the other twenty-four men with the same job description, were responsible for the operating, maintaining, and repairing of the ship's engines and generators, among other things. When we weren't doing that, we were supervising the operation of the boilers, keeping the bilges clean, or administering boiler water treatment chemicals.

Which was what I was doing when I overheard that there was yet *another* iceberg warning.

"That's six official warnings for icebergs since yesterday," I hear one of my crew members mutter to another.

I say mutter, but of course we all have to shout in here to be heard, the noise of the engines and constant mechanical *whirring* making it almost impossible to have a conversation.

And this is how I know that my colleagues are on edge about the warnings. Because we keep talk to a minimum down here. Only when it's necessary do we exert some of our precious energy on shouting back and forth to one another.

I finish up my work and make my rounds, making sure all is as it should be.

I just had my break, so I won't be free to seek out Chief Officer Bell until later today, possibly even tonight. But I make a mental note to speak to him as soon as I'm able.

Because six warnings may not be out of the ordinary for such a lengthy journey, but not to order the slowing down of the engines…surely that must be an oversight.

Michel

After dinner in the dining room, I take my boys back to our cabin in second-class, no. F4, and tuck them into their respective beds – Master on the bottom, Edmond on the top.

I'm glad to say that, since that first morning, Edmond has not woken up feeling nauseous, and I can only guess that he's found his sea legs.

But being sick or not, one thing remained a constant each night. My little boys missed their mama.

"Has she gotten lost?" Master asks me now, as I stroke his white-blond hair.

I sigh, take a moment to consider how best to answer.

"Mama is –"

"Is she with Edward?" Edmond interrupts me, leaning over the side of the bunk bed, and in an instant my guilt is washed away.

I clench my jaw, bend over to kiss Master on the forehead, then straighten up to tuck Edmond back in.

I don't answer them – which in and of itself is an answer – and I guess my sudden change in temperament is noticeable, because neither of them says another word.

I settle down on the sofa – not to sleep, it is too slim for my broad frame. But I cannot call it a night yet, not when my mind is racing a mile a minute.

It's almost unbelievable how much time I continue to waste on feeling guilty.

Marcelle had it coming. She and Edward deserve each other. I *shouldn't* feel this monumental remorse for what I did to her.

Which is why it kills me that I *do*.

Does this make me a better person than her? That I feel bad for what I've done, when she felt none for what she did?

But then again, what I did was so much worse…

The voice of reason which has been mocking me bubbles up like acid, and I press the flats of my palms against my temples.

I did the right thing.

I know I did.

My boys will grow up without their mother's depravity, with their father who would give up everything for them. Who *did* give up everything for them.

And who knows, maybe one day, when I divulge what I have done, they too will see that I had no other choice.

Catherine

There is a party in full swing when we make our way to dinner, and at the sound of the merry music, my family and I gravitated towards it like a moth to a flame.

The open space on D-deck is crammed full of people when we peer inside. The room is lit with an orange glow, cigarette smoke trailing around the lights. It smells of sweat, beer and cheer.

And I cannot help but grin widely at the spectacle.

"Can we dance?" I ask Father, bouncing with excitement as I turn to him, my hands clasped before me as if in prayer.

He didn't like us begging like that. _Like sad little puppies_, he'd always say.

But this time was different, I could tell by the glint in his eyes that he, too, wanted to forsake dinner for a bit of jolly fun.

He nodded his big head at me, a quick jut, and I don't wait around to hear Mother's response.

"Come on!" I say, grabbing William by the hand and pulling him into the crowd.

Everyone is either dancing, laughing, drinking, or smoking. Some do all four at once. The mood is contagious.

William and I snake our way through the crowd easily enough, our skinny little bodies fitting through the gaps without much bother. And then we are in the centre of the crowd, where a circle of people creates a space to dance and jump around.

A laugh bubbles out of me at the sight of fiddle players within the crowd, of people stomping their feet and clapping their hands in time with the musicians' tune.

A little girl younger than me is twirling around in the centre of the circle with an older man, his wrinkled face creased with a big, toothless grin.

"Come on!" I say to William again, hoping he'll join me. But he lets go of my hand as I stumble into the circle alone.

I look back at him and he's shaking his head, his expression sombre in a way I have never seen before.

He looks over my shoulder and I follow his gaze to a group of girls, the pretty brunette one he was talking to yesterday, at the front. She's playing with her long, straight hair and…I look back at William, then back at the girl…she's making eyes at my brother, and I know why he cannot be seen making a fool of himself.

Boys, I think, shaking my head. But I quickly shrug and turn to face the girl and the old man.

His loss, I think, and pick up my skirts to join in the dance.

I can hear my mother and father calling joyfully from the circle's edge as I jump around with many others, can hear my father's big bear hands clapping loudly to the beat, along with everyone else.

Then someone grabs my wrist. I look up to see my brother amid the dancing after all, and I find myself glad for it.

Dinner was forgotten, not my family nor I feeling the pinch of hunger in our stomachs as we frolicked, danced, and sung the night away.

For how could we? When our hearts were so full.

Victor

"They lack the manners," Maria is telling the Colonel now, as we watch the waiter pour our drinks.

"They may dress like us, travel like us, wine and dine like us, but the decorum fails to follow," she's saying.

I don't interrupt her because, ultimately, I don't disagree.

I don't dislike Margaret and James Brown. They are new money, certainly, but does that make them bad people? No. Of course not. And yet I do not feel compelled to come to their defence, because Mrs Brown insulted John Jacob Astor today, and I would use that to my advantage in creating a relationship with this man.

"To question the capability and discretion of Captain Edward Smith is simply ludicrous," the Colonel is saying in response to Maria's comment, while his new wife nods slowly beside him, "King Edward VII himself awarded him the Transport Medal in 1903. He is one of the world's most experienced sea captains. Did you know that he took command of the Olympic last year, back when it was the largest vessel in the world? Now, of course, the Titanic is."

He pauses to take a sip of his Scotch.

"I did not know that," I tell him, though I did of course. But in order to gain Astor's regard, I didn't mind pretending to be less knowledgeable than I was. If it made the man feel like he could teach me a few things, I'd happily let him think he was taking me under his wing.

His very rich wing. Probably made of gold –

"Indeed!" he says, "So to question his judgement," he shakes his head now, no doubt thinking of Margaret Brown's displaced horror at the shortage of lifeboats, "Well, it's unseemly."

"Quite," I agree, and we all fall silent for a moment.
I take a sip of my Cognac and watch the rest of the party over the rim of my glass as they do the same.
When my gaze drifts to Maria I throw a wink at her, and she playfully rolls her eyes at me in response.
She doesn't like to be here, mingling with John Jacob Astor and his 'little wife'. She'd made that perfectly clear all day following the Colonel's invitation this morning to meet them for a drink at the lounge after dinner.
But I wouldn't take no for an answer from Maria, the opportunity to rub elbows with such affluence being one of the main reasons *why* I had wanted to conclude our honeymoon on this prestigious ship.
Maria thinks she *made* me buy these tickets; thinks she pouted and I gave in, more than happy to please my new wife.
And while that was true, I do have a mind of my own…and I had my own reasons – aside from wanting to spoil Maria – to be here.
But I let her think she's doing me a favour. If there's one thing I know, it's never to let *anyone* see all your cards.

"Tell me, Madeleine," Maria is saying now, turning to the wife, and I smile to myself to hear her addressing her so informally, a great contrast to how she still addresses Margaret Brown.
Like me, Maria knows, at least, with whom to turn on the charm. And I love her all the more for it.
The women's chatter about their dress' designer – the Lady Duff Gordon – being a fellow passenger on the ship, becomes background noise to me, and I turn to the Colonel.

"What brings you on the Titanic's maiden voyage, John?" I ask, hoping to learn more about him.

Astor inhales, his eyebrows raised, "We were honeymooning in Europe."

"Ah! So were we," I say, as though I don't know that he and Madeleine had just recently married. Feigning ignorance from their very public scandal would serve me well.

Astor nods at me, "We hoped to be away longer but –"

I raise my glass to my lips, sip the soothing medicine, and give him all the time he needs.

With one sceptically raised eyebrow, Astor must deem me trustworthy enough, because a moment later he's confiding in me, "Madeleine is pregnant, you see?"

I nod and smile in congratulations, tip my crystal to his as though this is breaking news.

"Yes, thank you," he mumbles before continuing, "So we thought it best to return and get my affairs in order."

"Such as?" I ask. The question is risky, I knew, but I was two Cognac's deep by now, and my tongue was looser than I was used to.

But to my surprise, Astor does not seem fazed.

"Well, you know," he says matter-of-factly, "As a man of considerable wealth it's only right that I amend my will so that this child would have the same inheritance rights as my other children. Though they are all adults by now."

"Quite right, quite right," I say, nodding my head.

"Yes," Astor agrees – with himself I realise after a moment.

"It may ruffle some feathers," I hear myself say, and I inwardly kick myself.

But Astor's moustache twitches, and his eyes crinkle. He is smiling. And then he is laughing.

"I didn't think I could ruffle any more than I have already!"

I join in his laughter, which, to my delight, does not feel forced.

"As you can imagine, my ex-wife and my children by her were not best pleased when Madeleine and I wed," he says.

I nod and bite my tongue. I don't want to say the wrong thing, and right now my mind is not coming up with an appropriate reply.

"Do you have children?" the Colonel asks me now, moving on – thank heavens – and Maria and Madeleine turn their heads to rejoin the conversation, as if they had some kind of radar signalling that we had returned to a preferred topic of conversation. Women could be such odd creatures.

"Oh, not yet," Maria says, replying for me.

She flashes me a smile and I reach over and take her hand, kiss her knuckles, silently acknowledging our struggles.

"Soon," I promise, "I dare say we will be blessed soon. When we are returned home. When things are less hectic."

Madeleine was nodding slowly, then offered Maria a small smile, and I sensed a kinship between the women.

She may be young, I thought, *but Madeleine was perceptive.*

We henceforth fall into easy conversation, the four of us sharing entertaining stories from our travels around Europe. The alcohol was flowing, even Madeleine enjoying a couple of flutes of champagne.

But after a while I feel a gentle hand on my upper arm, and I know it's Maria's.

"Would you care for a nightcap back in our suite, darling?" her voice drips into my ear like a fine wine, and I know it is a warning as to my liquor limit. I turn to the sound.

"My beautiful wife, Colonel," I slur, "Always knows what I need before I need it."

I hear the Colonel and his wife titter amicably and I turn to see Astor peck his wife gently on the cheek.

"I bid you goodnight, my good fellow," I say, rising from my seat. Maria snakes her arm around mine casually, though I can feel that she is keeping me from swaying.

"Good night, sir," the Colonel says to me, "It was a pleasure. Perhaps we could arrange to meet for brunch tomorrow?"

"Brunch!" I reply, a little too excitedly, "Yes, tomorrow, eleven A.M."

He nods his head at me, "Fabulous," he says, "Until then."

"Until then," I reply, as Maria steers me away, and I *know* it is the start of a beautiful – and influential – friendship.

Except, I didn't know anything at all…

Ethel

It is late, and Edward and I are ready for bed.

After a lovely early dinner followed by a Sunday service, singing hymns in the saloon, we did not wish to socialise much more.

We've met some pleasant people on this trip, and it has been wonderful to hear so many of their stories, to learn what brought them here.

But Edward and I were both knackered, and by eleven P.M we are snuggled up in the bottom berth of our bunk bed, Edward's tall frame pressed against my back.

I don't know about him, but I fall asleep in an instant, my body relaxing in his warm embrace, my mind finding comfort as his fingers intertwine with mine and he holds me safely to him.

23:40

Thomas

I am talking to my colleague, Junior Assistant Fourth Engineer Arthur Ward, in Boiler Room 5 when we hear the bell ringing three times, interrupting our mundane chatter.
My eyes grow wide for a moment…and then an earthquake shakes the ground beneath us.
But of course, that cannot be…we are at sea…
We are knocked to the floor, a long, sharp grinding noise ripping through my ears, and I look around in a panic as the room shakes.
Before I even have time to ask Ward what has happened, I hear loud voices shouting frantically, and Ward and I turn to see our senior engineer, John Hesketh, and Leading Fireman Frederick Barrett, barrelling towards us.
They race at top speed through the connecting tunnel, their faces red and their eyes wide as they wave their arms before them wildly.
Suddenly it all dawns on me, and I am forced into action before my mind has even processed what must have occurred. I spring towards them just as they crash into Boiler Room 5, and together we lower the bulkhead doors.
"Impact!" Frederick Barrett shouts, "Starboard! Water pouring in two feet above the stokehold plates in Boiler Room 6, No.10 stokehold!"
Where the fire raged for two days after we set sail.
It is enough to kick us into high gear, and all four of us hurry into position to instruct the rest of the crew, adrenaline and fear pushing us forward.

Michel

I wake with a start and immediately press my hand to my stiff neck. I must have fallen asleep while reading on the sofa.

I sit up and stretch my neck one way and then the other, sighing gratefully when I hear the bone click.

I relax for a moment, allowing sleep to find me again, when I am suddenly stirred by the sound of footsteps running up and down outside our door.

I look to my sleeping sons, glad that whoever that is hasn't woken them with their thoughtlessness, and I head to the door to firmly request that they be quiet.

What I am faced with stuns me, my irritation quickly evaporating into confusion.

Several people are walking up and down the hallway, many others, like me, with their heads sticking out of their door and with their brows furrowed together in perplexion.

What is going on here?

I must have said it out loud because the fellow in the cabin next to ours looks towards me.

"Did you hear it, too?" he asks me.

"Hear what?"

He shakes his head, "It was like a scraping. Metal against metal, it sounded like."

I blink back at him, "I heard nothing."

But didn't I? Something must have woken me from my sleep. If not my cricked neck, then maybe a sound?

"Is there a reason for all this?" I ask now, waving my hand to the people hurrying past me.

A woman turns to me, and I see a look of pure panic in her eyes.
I swallow, retreat into my cabin, close the door.
I would like to investigate what is happening. But I can't very well leave my sons alone in here.
Taking a step away from the door, I get a sinking feeling in my stomach that something is wrong, and I instinctively look to our two small suitcases, still propped up on the floor by our dresser.
There's no need to unpack.
In case we need a quick getaway.
The thoughts from our first day onboard crash into my mind again, and I lick my dry lips before grabbing our few discarded items and flinging them into the cases.
"Papa?"
I hear Edmond's little voice behind me and turn to see him rubbing his eyes in the candlelight.
I open my mouth to automatically tell him to go back to sleep, but I stop myself, because something inside me is telling me we need to run.

Catherine

"Get up, children! Hurry, hurry!"
My mother's voice, and her hands, shakes me awake.
"Mother?" I mumble, wiping the side of my mouth where I know I have drooled, "What is it?"
She doesn't reply but when my eyes adjust to the light and my mind takes in the chaos, I am suddenly wide awake.
My father is stuffing things into our small bags, his head snapping from side to side in search of things. He's barking orders at Alice and at Mother, who are scurrying back and forth around the small cabin.
Their urgency is terrifying.
"Put this on," my mother tells me now, shoving a threadbare scarf at me while Alice hangs out the door and peers outside.
"What's going on, Mother?" I hear myself say, and I look to William beside me, who, too, has been told to dress warmly.
His big, blue eyes are wide with terror as he meets my gaze, and I see my own fear reflected back at me in their shine.
Crying. It is not something I am used to seeing my big brother do.
Then he shakes his head at me ever so slightly and swallows his tears.

Victor

"What was that?" Maria whispers, her grip on my shoulders digging into me for a second.

I continue to thrust over her, "What? Nothing," I grunt.

But I can feel she is no longer in the moment, her eyes searching the room.

I roll off her with an irritated sigh, cover my face with my arm.

"You could have at least let me finish," I grumble. And I mean it.

So selfish.

But she is not paying me any attention, instead pushing off the bed and throwing a silk robe around herself.

She pads towards the door as she ties the lace around her waist.

"Maria…don't presume to open that door in your state of undress," I warn her.

To my surprise, she ignores me, turning the door handle and sticking her head outside.

"Maria!" I exclaim, jumping off the bed and hurrying towards her, uncaring about my complete nakedness, as long as it meant nobody saw her partial exposure.

I slam the door closed in her face.

"What is the matter with you?" I scold.

"Didn't you feel it?" she whispers, her beautiful brown eyes meeting mine.

I frown. What is she worried about?

We are on the Unsinkable Titanic!

What could possibly happen?

I am about to sigh in irritation, when her expression stops me. Her eyes are wide, and I'm taken aback to see her like this. She is scared. And her fear sobers me up

"Do you want me to go enquire?" I ask now, matching her tone, my frustration gone in a second to see her so vulnerable. She nods her head at me quickly, a hand coming up to the base of her throat.

My gaze drifts to her hand. It is shaking.

I dress quickly, picking up my discarded clothes off the floor.

Then I'm by the door, "I'll be back in a moment," I tell her, before slipping out into the well-lit hallway.

There are a few people hurrying about, men and women frowning at each other as they try to make sense of what they heard and felt.

I hurry down the staircase to the first-class lobby, looking around myself. Some people are outside on the deck, I follow them.

The cold bites into me, and I shove my hands into my pockets. A fellow walks past me, looking up, while the lady on his arm looks over the railing into the dark water.

I follow the man's gaze, see nothing out of the ordinary.

What is going on?

It appears no one knows.

I turn to head back inside in search of someone who might give me some better insight.

It doesn't take me long to find a steward.

"Excuse me!" I call to him.

The man in a white uniform turns around, a smile plastered on his lips. I can tell it's not sincere.

"My wife and I felt a bump," I explain, "Is there something wrong?"

Almost immediately, the steward raises his hands, palms facing me, and breathes a little laugh, "Oh no, sir. Nothing is wrong." I raise my chin slightly, automatically accepting his reply. But the frown between my brows remains.

Quickly – too quickly – the man excuses himself, turns, and hurries along on his way.

I look around myself again. More people have left their cabins and are congregating outside on the boat deck, many leaning over the side in the hopes of seeing – what? I don't know.

But I do not like this.

And my gut is telling me to protect Maria. At all costs.

Ethel

I wake with a jolt.

"Edward?" I say into the near darkness.

It must still be night, because when I look outside our small, round window, I can see the black curtain of the sky, dotted with tiny specks of starlight.

"What is it, darling?" Edward asks, stirring beside me.

I can't see him, but I feel his fingers finding my face, then cupping my cheek.

I take his hand in mine and squeeze it before settling back down.

"Nothing," I say after a moment, closing my eyes again, "I thought I heard something."

There's a knock at our door and Edward is up in a flash.

"What on Earth…" he mutters as he grabs a robe and shoves his arms through.

I prop myself up on one elbow, blinking furiously in hopes of adjusting my eyes to the shadows.

I feel like I've only just fallen asleep, but surely that cannot be. Why would somebody be knocking on our cabin in the middle of the night?

There was another knock before Edward had even managed to reach the door, and by now I was beginning to feel frantic.

I sit up, pull the sheets to my chest. Not out of modesty, but unease. What was going on?

"I'm coming, I'm coming," Edward calls to whoever is knocking, before twisting the door handle and pulling it open.

DAY FIVE

MIDNIGHT

Harold Cottam

I would have missed the call if not by mere chance.

I was already unlacing my boots, done for the night just a few minutes after midnight, and while I did this, I had kept my apparatus on.

Just by chance.

Had the call come even five minutes later, I would have missed it.

"Come at once!" I hear my good friend Jack Phillip's voice call through the headpiece, "We have struck a berg. It's a CQD old man."

"Is it serious?" I hear myself ask, dumbfounded to be receiving such a message from the Titanic.

"Yes, it's a CQD!" he calls back, "Here's the position, report it, and get here as soon as you can!"

I didn't waste any time.

If the *Unsinkable* Titanic was asking for immediate assistance, then lives were at risk. And given the fact the coordinates he gave were a good sixty miles away, I knew it would take us on the Carpathia at least four hours to get there…

I hastily climb down the ladder, hopping the last few rungs in my hurry, nearly stumbling in my haste, and seeing a light on in the captain's cabin, I knock quickly before bursting in.

"Who the hell!?" he exclaims, his brow furrowed though he will instinctively know that my intrusion must mean something serious.

"The Titanic has struck ice, sir!" I report, "She is in distress! I have her position here."

He snatches the paper from me, "Give it here then!" and stands up.

With a quick glance at the coordinates, Captain Arthur Rostron and I race out of his cabin.

"We are about four hours away from her position," I tell him as we climb the ladder.

"Wake the crew," he orders me, "Have them organise food, blankets, and medical care for any survivors."

And I speed away while the captain barks orders at the few officers nearby to increase Carpathia's speed to her maximum potential.

Thomas

"The water is pouring in! It has risen fourteen feet above the keel in the first five compartments since impact," Bell shouts above the noise of the machinery and the men grunting as they shovel coal.

"Two hours!" another shouts.

My head snaps up. As do several others', before we remember we cannot stop.

"It is our duty, gentlemen, to remain at our stations!" Bell calls to us all, "It is up to us to keep her afloat for as long as possible, to allow for the passengers to board the lifeboats."

The lifeboats.

The few we have.

"How many souls on board, sir?" I hear one of the men yell.

"Including us crew, just under two-thousand-three-hundred," Bell calls back into the crowd, answering the unspoken question we are all asking.

There aren't enough lifeboats. Not for the passengers. And certainly not for the crew.

No one replies. We all know what it means: that most would die. And all we could do was give the passengers a little more time.

We are ordered here and there, some of us sent to operate the pumps in the forward compartments, others off to keep the generators running to maintain power and lights throughout the ship. A handful of others and I were sent to keep the steam up in the boiler rooms that weren't already submerged. I try not to think of the poor sods who are already dead, floating in the flooded Boiler Rooms 6 and 5 – the rooms and bulkhead that were damaged, its metal likely weakened by the fire…

Our efforts, for as long as we can hold, will keep the ship above water. Every one of us has a part to play in saving lives. At the very likely expense of our own.

I push these thoughts aside as I race to my station, as well as the thoughts of my two boys as they begin to creep in.

I cannot think of them now. It would not aid me one bit to break down.

All I could do right now was to do my job.

That, and pray.

Michel

I scoop Edmond out of the bed and sit him on the sofa. I push a jumper over his head and stuff his feet into his tiny shoes.

"Papa?" his little voice croaks, "Is it morning?"
I don't answer him, instead turning to wake up Master.

"Master," I say gently, coaxing him from sleep, "*Allez*," and then he's in my arms.
I plop him beside his younger brother, "I'm still tired!" Master whines.
I shove his little arms through the sleeves of his jacket, push a hat over both their heads.

"I want to go back to sleep!" Master complains again, tears beginning to well in his eyes, and something in me snaps.

"I need you both to be strong," I tell them as I take Master's face in my hands. They engulf almost his entire head, and I realise with a clenching in my stomach that I am asking too much of them.
They must feel my worry, because suddenly Edmond is crying, his mouth opened wide, and his head thrown back as he gasps loudly for air.

"I want mama!" he shouts, and I die a little inside.
Master's lip is quivering beside Edmond.
Suddenly there's a swift knock on the door and it's opened before I even turn around.

"I heard crying," says the man from the cabin next to ours.
Scraping. Like metal against metal.

"

I should be disturbed by this stranger's sudden entry into our space, but I know there's something sinister underfoot, so I gratefully accept his intrusion.

"My sons…" I say, and before I know it, the man is already kneeling down before Master and putting on his shoes for him. I realise he is offering me a kindness, helping me as I travel alone with two small children.

"Are you by yourself?" I ask.

He shakes his head, "My wife is packing our things."

"Have we arrived, papa?" Master's voice squeaks.

The man stands up and together we look down at my babies.

"Yes," I hear myself say, "Yes, Master, Mon. We have arrived, and it is time to leave."

At that, Edmond hops off the sofa and takes my hand.

"Will we see mama now?"

The lump in my throat is so big I can barely breathe, nevermind answer.

The man must sense my horror, because he quickly takes Master by the hand and heads out the door, "I am sure you and your mama will soon be reunited."

Catherine

I still don't know what is going on, but I can sense it isn't good.

There is a lot of shouting and pushing all around us as we try to navigate through a maze of corridors thick with people.

The stewards must have alerted my parents, because I can see them ahead knocking and opening other people's cabins, shouting instructions to put on the life vests.

I look down at mine, then to William's. Father has one too, and Mother. Only Alice is without.

"Alice doesn't have a life vest, Father!" I call to the head of our group.

He turns around, looks at me, then at Alice behind.

"We will get her one," my father says, "Don't you worry."

I nod, assured by the certainty in his voice.

We are all trying to head upstairs. That much I know.

Father is pushing his way past some people now, or at least trying to. But all the men have the same idea, and they are all in the same hurry.

We are a chain, my family and I: Father at the front holding a case in one hand, Mother's hand in the other as she follows behind. She is holding William's hand, and I William's, and lastly Alice behind me.

We reach a staircase and make our way up.

Someone forces their way ahead of us, a man and a woman, pushing past us as best they can as the woman carries a little baby in her arms and the man carries a toddler.

My father sees them and for a second I think he's going to block their path. But he does a quick double take and then presses his broad frame against the wall, allowing them priority.

"Mother," I pipe up now that we have stopped, "I'm scared." I don't know what I was expecting. A word of reassurance? A calming smile?

But when she turns to face me, I only see alarm.

"Gates!" I hear someone shout ahead of us, and we all crane our necks to see.

Being third class passengers meant that we were separated from certain areas intended only for second or first-class passengers. These areas were made off-limits by waist-high gates, which weren't always closed, but as I strain my neck to see, I notice they have been secured during the night.

"We can make it over," I hear Father say as he turns to face Mother, "Com' on, I'll take Will. You take Cat. Alice!?"

"I can make it," I hear Alice reply from behind me as Mother reaches over and pulls me to her.

She grabs under my armpits and lifts me up into her arms, holding me in a way she hasn't done in years.

"I've got you, baby," she tells me as I wrap my thin arms around her neck.

I look at her, the many people around us shouting, pushing and climbing over the gate, and I finally see the comfort I needed, the look in her eyes promising me that I am safe.

As long as my mother is with me, I know that I am safe.

Victor

I return to our suite to tell Maria to dress and am glad to see she is already doing so.

"I'll get Fermina," I tell her, and turn back around to knock on the maid's room across the hall from us.

I stand waiting outside her door for a whole two seconds before knocking again.

Finally, I hear movement and shuffling of feet.

"Mina!" I call, "*Ándale!*"

The door opens a crack.

"*Que pasa?*"

"Pack your bags," I tell her, "Then come to us and help Maria."

The tone of my voice tells her it is serious, and she quickly turns to do as I asked.

Just before I re-enter our suite, I spot three stewards hurrying down the hallway, knocking on doors to rouse the sleeping passengers.

Nothing is wrong, eh?

Inside our suite, I find Maria fastening her a fur around her shoulders.

"What was it?" she asks me.

I shake my head, "I don't know," then grab a few belongings, stuff them into a case.

"Victor," Maria calls me from across the room. I don't look up.

"Victor!" she calls again, and I cannot bear to hear the sound of her fear.

I raise my head, meet her gaze.

"Nothing will happen to you," I tell her firmly.

"To *us*," she corrects, a hand at her throat as she tries to remain calm.

I nod at her once, then return to packing.

"Come," I say after a moment, grabbing hold of the one case. I'm not even sure what I threw in there. Nothing material mattered. It could all be replaced.

I take hold of Maria's hand and head to the door just as Mina opens it and steps inside.

She's carrying the one lonely little case she boarded with.

"Stewards are waking people," she tells us, "They say to head to the boat deck."

I clench my jaw and nod at her.

"Let's go," I tell them.

Maria takes a quick scan of the room, but I grab her hand, guide her out the door, "We have no use for anything else."

As we make our way through the hallway, I notice more urgency from our fellow guests than I did twenty minutes ago when I first came out to check.

They are all heading one way now, no more back and forth in confusion, one steward leading the way as the others remain behind, I presume to help any elderly, or passengers with young children.

"This way," I tell the ladies, following the crowd. We look like a school of fish.

Maria squeezes my hand tightly. And together we head towards the boat deck, and the unknown.

00:25

Ethel

Thanks to the man in the cabin next to ours warning us of what he'd seen with his own eyes – that the ship had barely missed barrelling into an enormous iceberg – Edward and I were outside before most.

We arrived on the boat deck twenty minutes ago, just in time to see some of the crew hastily uncovering the lifeboats and checking their provisions.

We assumed they would be asking people to board them immediately, but to my amazement, we are still standing around like statues, impatiently waiting for word as the crew hurry up and down shouting orders at one another.

The band began to play shortly after we appeared, the very men we saw playing by the library just yesterday, arranging themselves on deck with their instruments. And now their jolly music fills the air, a great contrast to the throbbing numbness in my chest.

"Surely any minute now?" Edward breathes frustratedly beside me as he stomps his booted feet to keep the blood circulating. His words form a white mist before his pale face.

I shiver, with cold or with trepidation, I no longer know. Edward reaches his arm around me and rubs my shoulder.

Suddenly there is a loud *zipping* sound followed by a *bang*. We look up to see a splash of colour in the black sky.

"What's that?" I whisper, though I think I know.

Edward swallows, his Adam's apple bobbing, "It is the distress signal."

I notice then, that the crowd around us has multiplied exponentially in the time we've been waiting. I wouldn't have known it from the sound, as everyone is being strangely quiet. Only the band's rendition of 'Oh, You Beautiful Doll' suggests we are even here.

The calm before the storm.

I look around at all these stranger's faces, some old, some young, some wrapped up with scarves and hats, others less prepared.

My gaze rests on a woman and her three children, all of them shivering before her. I smile at the youngest, a little black-haired boy with big green eyes. He doesn't smile back, and I don't blame him. This eery silence among the chaos has got to be the most unnerving occurrence I, too, have ever experienced.

Thomas

We have seventy-three coal trimmers, twenty-five engineers including myself, thirteen leading firemen, thirty-three greasers, and eight electricians, and together we are doing all that we can to keep her afloat.

We operate the pumps in the forward compartments and keep the steam up in the boiler rooms that have not yet been consumed by the sea.

But it's a losing battle, and we all know it.

"Millar," Chief Officer Bell's voice calls from behind me.

I turn around.

"Wife?" he barks at me.

I shake my head, "Deceased, sir."

He clenches his jaw, as though to chew on my answer, and with it he nods briskly and walks away.

I return to my work and wonder if I should have told him about my sons…

But it wouldn't have mattered.

Because at this time he was rounding up those of us who had a wife back at home, the first to be dismissed to try to reach the boat deck.

Everyone had someone. Everyone would have a child, a mother, a cousin, a partner. And this was how those in charge managed to dismiss us in sections.

Those of us who have a wife waiting for them, they may leave soon.

But for those who are not so lucky…well, we stay.

Michel

"Women and children!"

"Women and children, please step forward!"

The announcement chills me to my bones.

"Women and children to board the lifeboats first!"

Master, Edmond, and I are among a crowd of people, my hands firmly holding onto theirs so that I do not lose them in the confusion.

At the officer's call, many sound out in distress, women turning into their husbands, their fathers, their grandfathers, unwilling to be separated.

A lump forms in my throat as an elderly couple in front of me holds each other so tightly I can see the woman's knuckles turning white, like the hand of a skeleton.

"Women and children, please!" the officer calls again.

I hang back.

I need to think.

"Papa?" Master's little voice calls to me and I look down at his face.

His round cheeks, big eyes, and red nose are all I see, so tightly have I wrapped them against the chill.

"*Oui?*" I say to him, forcing a smile to my face.

But he doesn't say anything, instead dropping his gaze back before him.

All he sees from down there are the backs of people's trousers as they begin to shuffle forward, and I wonder how much he understands.

Nothing, I'd wager. And for a brief moment I feel relief flooding me. In this moment of great uncertainty and fear, I thank God that my sons are too young to understand the enormity of our situation.

I watch from among the crowd as lifeboat 7 slowly fills up with women and children, some weeping silently, others making themselves comfortable on the small boat.

Overhead, rockets are being blasted into the air, and I look down at my two and four-year old boys. They are mesmerised by the red and orange colours breaking apart the blanket of black that is this cold April night.

I observe their expressions, so calm in the face of danger.

In fact, everyone is being weirdly calm, considering we are performing an evacuation in the middle of the Atlantic.

Some gentlemen pace up and down the deck, smoking their pipes or looking around, but largely the crowd is still and silent. A call from an officer snaps my attention back to the lifeboat. He is waving his arms up and down to his colleagues. The boat is lowering.

I count twenty-eight people aboard.

"There is more room!" I hear someone shout from among the crowd, followed by much agreement, mine included.

"Bring more women and children forward!"

But the officers ignore our outcries, and the lifeboat goes down and out of sight, into safety.

We made it over the first gate and continued to make our way up to the boat deck.

The white hallways are a maze!

I'm holding Father's hand now as he propels me forward for a time, but I quickly lose my footing one too many times, and before I know it, he has hauled me into his big arms.

I notice then that our case is gone, and I point this out to him.

"Don't worry 'bout it," he mumbles, "It's not important."

I wonder briefly what was inside it as I hold on tightly, but the thought is quickly dismissed as we turn another sharp corner.

"Another gate!" Father calls to Mother, William and Alice behind us.

I turn my head to where he is looking just as three men are climbing over it. Two turn left, another turns right, and I wonder who we should follow.

Father drops me down over the waist-high gate and I stand back to give the rest of my family space.

Mother climbs over first, her skirts bunched up around her thighs, Father holding her hand. Alice follows closely behind, the same process as with Mother. Then Father picks William up under his arms and swings him over. I take my brother's hand, and he looks down at me.

"It'll be okay, Cat," he tells me.

Father is the last one over and then his head snaps left to right, before making a decision, "This way," he says.

Then we all begin to race down the hall, and I realise we turned the same way the one lone man did before us.

Victor

We pass through the first-class lobby and out onto the boat deck directly in front of lifeboat 8.

At the sound of upbeat music, I turn to see the ship band strumming their instruments. How odd to see them out here, and not in the saloon.

"What's happening?" Maria asks me, her wide eyes searching the scene before us.

We all stand aside and watch as the officers wave people forward.

All I can hear is the abysmal music from the band, and it's making my head throb.

"*Que pasa?*" Fermina asks now, her voice hitching into hysteria.

I shake my head as I continue to watch the people, some climbing into lifeboats, some standing back.

Nothing was making sense to me. None of it.

This was the *unsinkable* Titanic, for God's sake!

"Excuse me?"

The voice beside me snaps me out of my frenzy.

"Countess of Rothes," Maria says, recognising the woman.

The lady looks completely out of place in her big feather hat and emerald green dress. All she has for warmth is a flimsy shawl.

She reaches for Maria's arm, squeezes it.

"They are boarding women and children first," the countess tells us.

I nod at her, glad to finally know what to do.

"Women and children?" Maria parrots.

The countess nods, then heads towards the lifeboat.

Mina takes Maria's hand, "Come, *dona*," but Maria shrugs her off.

"No!" she cries suddenly, throwing her arms around my neck. I stand frozen in shock, so still I don't even embrace her, my arms hanging limply at my sides, "Nononononono," she whimpers.

Maria is sobbing into my shirt, "Victor, I won't go without you."

I snap out of my state at her remark, "Yes you will!" I tell her, taking her firmly by the arms.

I try to pry her off me so that I can look into her eyes, one more time. But her grasp on my jacket is too tight, her face pressed into my chest.

A lump forms in my throat, one I cannot afford to let disperse into tears. I have to be strong for Maria now. Because if I show even a hint of fear, I know she will never board that damn lifeboat.

As she continues to cry, I look to Mina, who is frantically looking back and forth between us and the lifeboat which would save her.

I realise I have but a moment to persuade her to depart without me. My arms relax around Maria, reaching around to hold her to me now as her sobs sound above the ridiculous music.

I press a kiss to the top of her head, and she finally raises her gaze to meet mine.

"I am the nephew of King Alfonso XIII's prime minister," I remind her with a sure smile, "I will find a way onto a lifeboat, my darling. And I will find you when we are rescued," I grin at her, "You know money will get you anywhere."

00:45

Ethel

The distress signals are being fired every five minutes as we watch the women and children being ushered onto lifeboats.

I feel sick at the thought of boarding without Edward. Feel sick at the thought of saying goodbye when we have only *just* come together.

We watch in silence as the woman with her three children are safely seated on the small craft, the little black-haired boy tucked neatly onto her lap, the other two bookending her, a thin blanket spread over their knees.

They are all wearing life vests, the officers having passed them out earlier.

I am wearing mine, but some people are still without – including Edward – the officers running up and down to procure more.

"You will go on the next one," Edward's voice says beside me then, the first thing either of us has said in the longest time. I look up at him and shake my head, part my chapped lips to refuse, but his cold shivering fingers come up to my face.

"I will find you afterwards, when we are rescued."

"No, Edward," I mumble, moving away from him, "We stick together."

He raises his head at the call of the officer announcing, "Life vests!" and reaches his long arm over me to grab one before they are all taken.

I watch him as he quickly pulls it over his head and ties the string around his middle.

"More women and children!" the officer at the front calls, to which many move forward, some women crying as they are ripped from the arms of their loved ones who did not qualify as worthy to save.

Tears begin to form in my eyes, but I quickly dash them away with the back of my hand, anger overriding my sadness.

"No!" I proclaim to my husband then, "You and I will *both* get on the next lifeboat."

"Ethel –"

"Hear me when I say this Edward," I protest, "You either climb on the boat with me, or be prepared to see me stay behind with you. One way or the other, we are not separating."

Suddenly a low moan erupts from all around us, like that of a whale beneath the surface, so long, loud, and eery that it can only be the ship itself.

I hastily grab hold of Edward, my feet no longer able to stay firmly planted in place, and a shared gasp escapes my fellow passengers as we all look about ourselves in panic.

"The bow is submerging!" we all hear an officer call, "Pick up your pace!"

It was then that the communal calm was disrupted, and many who had previously stood back and allowed the women and children ahead, pushed their way towards the nearest barge.

I am in Edward's arms suddenly, as he shields me from the stomping herd, both of us watching in shock.

Men are grabbing onto the ropes of the lifeboats, trying to climb on, children are crying out in fear, officers are shouting over the top, trying to be heard, trying to regain authority.

But all common sense has gone. We are no longer human beings looking out for one another.

Fear has reduced us to our most basic of instincts, the instinct to survive. We are suddenly no more than animals.

There was not much else we could do.

We maintain the ship as best we can. We've rigged the suction hoses, retained the generators, kept our cool when the world as we know it is sinking into the depths of Hell.

But the watertight bulkhead between Boiler Rooms 5 and 6 has succumbed to the water pressure, and has given way, leading to the bow's submersion.

Despite the chaos that surrounds us – all of us moving further back as each compartment of the ship is engulfed – it is the groaning and creaking of the vessel as it sinks that causes me the greatest distress.

It sounds otherworldly, ghostly. And I know that if I survive this, that the sound will forever haunt my subconscious.

If I survive this.

We all continue as best we can with our duties as the ship's incline becomes more prominent, some of us crying silently, others stone-faced as we meet our fears head on.

A lot of us have been released, Officer Bell having cleared those with wives and children back at home to attempt reaching the lifeboats.

I, too, have been dismissed…but I don't see how any of them will make it. Climbing the steep ladders from down here was a difficult enough task at the best of times, but with the ship trimming forward by the head will make climbing the ladders almost impossible.

Nevermind the fact that we are so far from the boat deck. Even third-class passengers will still be struggling, I'd wager – what with the many gates and the chaos, not to mention the flooded sections blocking their path.

It is why I have not left my post.

I look around at the few dozens of us left behind, labouring to keep her from going under that much quicker, labouring to give those above deck even another few minutes to save themselves. They are all heroes, these men. All of them. Even those who have been discharged and chosen to make a run for it.

And I am honoured to be among them.

In sporadic moments of weakness, I allow myself to think of Thomas and William, of their bright shining faces when I brought them to view the magnificent Titanic last year. The sheer pride in their eyes to know their father had helped to build it. This beast of great success in our time.

I think of William's little eyes twinkling when I gave them those coins, my farewell gift to them.

My stomach clenches to think of my parting words to them.

Don't spend it until my return.

Until my return.

My return.

Will that ever come to pass now?

I think of Jennie. Not of the final memory I have of her, pale and gaunt, but of a time when she was well, full of life.

She was so beautiful. An angel on Earth.

I still don't know what she ever saw in me, her kindness and earnestness a great contrast to my generally moody disposition, my easy distrust of people. Her laugh curls around me like smoke now as I allow my mind to drift to a better time, a better place. When we were happy. When we were all together.

Something we would never again be, even *if* I make it home.

If.

Such a fragile word. So small and yet it holds such power, like a scale destined to tip either way at the slightest change.

If.

If I make it home, I vow now, I will never leave my sons again, whether in body or in spirit. For too long I have been a husk of my former self, and they deserve so much more than that.

I vow to be that – much more – for my sons, if I return. To be a father of merit, if God wills it.

If He wills it.

If.

If…

The officer in charge, Lightoller I believe someone called him earlier, has ordered the crew to perform a locked-arm circle around the lifeboats so that only women and children could get through.

Panic had begun to take hold of people's hearts, several men having tried to force their way onto the boat.

I wasn't one of those men. I wouldn't dare to create such a ruckus, and risk frightening my children.

Instead, I remained further back, watching the madness unfold as I held my boys close. And I prayed that *any moment now* they would announce that men would be allowed to board the lifeboats. Perhaps even just those who, like myself, were travelling alone with younglings…

The shouting has become more intense, the band less audible over the commotion. Edmond has already cried out twice, once when someone bumped into us on their frantic way past, another time when one of the fire rockets *popped* right over our heads.

But they were both still now, the two of them being so very *very* good.

Or maybe frozen in terror.

I swallow the fear that threatens to take over, squash it down with the knowledge that they can sense my moods – as though they were a physical apparition that appears before them.

Papa is angry.

Papa is tired.

And worst of all, *Papa is scared.*

I wouldn't allow them to become infected with my own worries. It would serve them, me, us, naught.

Another lifeboat goes down. Another boat filled with only half its capacity.

I look around myself, the frown of doubt etched between my brows now a constant feature. Were there more lifeboats we did not know about? More, perhaps, in storage?

Why else would they not be filling each and every spot?

"Papa?"

Master calls me now, his little face looking up at me.

His nose is bright red, a beacon amid the snowy planes that are his cheeks.

I kneel down to his level, chuck him gently under the chin, "Yes, buddy?" I ask him, my forced smile firmly back in place.

"I'm cold," he tells me, as though his trembling chin and frosted fingers weren't signs enough.

I unravel my scarf from around my neck and wrap it around his. It swamps him, so I bind it around once, twice, until only his eyes are peeking out from underneath.

A chuckle escapes me at the adorable sight, and it feels both freeing and out of place.

"Better?" I ask, and he rewards me with the tiniest nod.

I turn to my baby, my two-year-old, who's behaving as though he were at least four times that age.

"How about you, Mon? You cold?"

Edmond only nods at me from underneath his hat and scarf.

I have nothing to give him except my own body heat, so I pick him up and hold him to me. With one arm under his buttocks for support, I use my free hand to rub his back.

"Just a little while longer, *mes chéris,*" I promise them, "Just a little while longer and we will all get on together."

Catherine

"This way, I'm sure it's this way."

My father was muttering underneath his breath, no longer talking to us, but to himself.

I was tired, so tired. We'd been running up and down the same white hallways for what felt like an age, turning back once after we realised we'd met a dead end.

A man, the lone man I'd seen take a right at the gate, ran past us at one point. My head had snapped round to watch him barrel past, and I wondered if I should tell Father that I saw him go this way earlier, that he likely encountered no exit.

But I didn't tell him, too scared was I to be wrong. For surely, the man would have warned us if that was the case…wouldn't he?

As it turned out, he wouldn't. And he didn't. And we faced the same metal wall he, too, must've come across ten minutes before.

Now we were racing back the way we came, my father cursing angrily when we moved past the very gate we had climbed over twenty minutes ago.

We could hear the ship moaning and creaking as we went. Sometimes I could hear a *pop* and would look around, sure that the walls were breaking apart all around us.

We've reached more stairs now, and we take them two at a time. At the top, I am gasping for air.

"Come on," Alice says beside me, taking my hand.

I look up at her and see a smile tugging at her lips. But her eyes are wet and red, and the smile does not reach them.

I realise it is for my benefit, to reassure me that all will be well. I press my lips together and give her a nod, taking one big gulp of air and pressing forward. I will carry on for my family, will *not* be a burden to their escape.

And with Alice's hand in mine, I pick up my skirts and keep on running.

Victor

Maria had to be pried from me. Physically pried off me. By an officer and the Countess of Rothes.

The whole thing had been traumatising, to watch her be manhandled and torn from me for her own safety. As if I was the very anchor that would drag her down.

I never broke eye contact with her as she was forced onto lifeboat 8, and only allowed myself to be pushed back into the crowd of other unfortunate men when I was sure she was safe and comfortable.

I watched as Mina covered her shoulders with a blanket and the countess took her hand, and I presented Maria with a smile that told her *Don't worry about me.*

A woman moves gingerly past me now, bumping me with her shoulder.

"Oh," she says, and I turn to see she is carrying a newborn baby in the crook of her arm and holds a tiny toddler by the hand.

"Here," I say, turning to allow her easier access to the boat. I hold her by the elbow and hover a hand over her lower back, carefully watching her footing as she climbs on, then turn to the little girl and pick her up, carefully placing her beside her mother.

"*Merci,*" the little girl mumbles at me, before taking a seat beside her mother, opposite Maria and Fermina. The woman, like Maria, is staring back at someone left behind, and I follow her gaze to a frail old man who I assumed to be her father. He was blowing them kisses, his wrinkly hand going back and forth from his lips to the space between them. His creased eyes are watery, and I wonder if it's from old age or sheer misery.

I look back at the woman and her babies; she is crying. An ugly cry of heartbreak. The little blond girl beside her is staring, petrified, into the distance as she clings onto her mother's frock.

I look away, my heart unable to take in any more sorrow – my own is already too much – and I return my attention back to my wife.

She, too, is violently crying, and I'm glad she's wedged in between Mina and the countess, for I'm sure she'd attempt an escape if she were not.

It is 1 a.m. when the lifeboat is sufficiently filled, and when the officer lets out a shout behind me to drop it, I step away. Lifeboat 8 is lowered into the black water, and as it descends, I think about how I had planned to spend my whole life with my beautiful wife. When we married just over eighteen months ago, it was what I had promised her: to spend the rest of my life with her. And it dawns on me then, as I watch her going further and further away from me, that in a sick kind of sense, I already have.

I exhale a shaky breath and take comfort in knowing that the further away from me Maria gets, the less likely she is to feel the terror reverberating off of me. Terror born from the sudden decision that I will not be using my status and power to weasel my way out of here, as I'd planned.

I may have a roll of cash tucked in my breast pocket. May have had every intention of using it to buy myself a space on board one of these godforsaken lifeboats.

But helping that woman and her small children on board had made me witness just *who* I would be taking that space from:

some innocent baby with their whole lives ahead of them, terrified and confused and unable to save themselves.

I could not be the reason why a young child did not escape this catastrophe. I would not.

And I realise, much too late in my privileged life, that regardless of wealth or pedigree, I was no more deserving of that space than the next person.

01:15

The ship lurches and the entire world screams.
I hold onto Edward's sleeve, narrowly falling onto an elderly couple beside us.

"Here!" Edward exclaims, stepping back and grabbing onto a railing, "hold on!"
I do as I'm told, one hand holding tightly onto the freezing metal rail, the other clasping Edward's as he holds me around my waist.

"You're getting on the next one!" he orders me.

"Not without –"
Suddenly we hear a gunshot! Was it really a gunshot?
But then another, and another. And I am certain I heard right. My eyes search the crowd, up and down on the higher deck trying to find the source of the sound.

"GET BACK!" I hear an officer shout, and my head snaps back to the lifeboats.
I see a wisp of smoke and follow it down to the shooter as the crowd around him disperses, several people holding up their hands, palms facing forward in surrender.

"Women and children ONLY!" the officer shouts, "There will be women and children only at this time!"
Warning shots.
No one is hurt. Not yet.

"Go on," Edward tells me, the gunshots quickly forgotten in the midst of such horror, "Get on."
But he continues to hold onto my waist, and I do not step out of his embrace.

Thomas

We're trapped in a steel tomb.

Boilers not required to supply steam for the pumps and dynamos have since been shut down. Keeping them under pressure was dangerous with the icy water coming in fast, and the last thing we needed now was an explosion from within.

It is utter chaos in the engine and boiler rooms, men shouting orders, running, some muttering prayers under their breath.

We all know we cannot *save* the ship. But every minute counts, and it is our duty to delay her from going under until help arrives. It is our only hope.

By now, the liner has trimmed forward significantly, the water seeping in at a phenomenal speed.

The noises from the ship as she strains is unsettling.

The steam and smoke all around us is choking us. And for a moment, I do not know which peril will kill me first.

Of course, we all want to flee. Our instinct to survive is *screaming*. But we also know what is required of us, what our duty was when we took this position. It is up to us to maintain the electrical lighting and the pumping of the water for the passengers and our fellow seamen.

We want to live. We want to get back to our families.

But in order for *everyone else* on board to have that possibility, we must stay on until the bitter end.

Catherine

We are running with the water. I can hear it sloshing under Father's feet with each hurried step.

He's carrying me again, and I cannot help but cry loud sobs into his ear.

"Mother!" William calls now as he stumbles, his hands and knees splashing in the icy water to break his fall.

He cries out and we all stop, turn.

I watch as Mother bends down and hauls him back up by his elbow, "It's okay, it's okay," she tells him calmly.

We carry on.

William is shivering, though we have been running forever.

We jumped two more gates, one of which was being held up by three stewards claiming we could not pass.

Father had punched one square in the face without hesitation and grabbed the other by the collar. I would've been scared by the outburst under normal circumstances.

But these were not normal circumstances.

The remaining steward fled following the beating of his colleagues, allowing us, and the half dozen other people, to scramble over.

The others, all adults, have steamed ahead, but my family is slower. William and I are struggling to keep up. Struggling to stay calm.

"Which way?" Alice says now as we stop at a crossroads.

The sign on the wall tells us left to the elevators. We follow it and find them already ankle deep with water. And empty.

"Back, back," Father instructs, "There will be a staircase."

With Mother at the lead now, we barrel back the way we came, the water now to our knees.

I am crying loudly, tears and snot running down my face. I have never been this scared in my entire life.

Not when I lost Mother at the park one day.

Not when I broke father's precious radio – the new one he'd *just* bought after the bailiffs repossessed the other one.

Not when William had scarlet fever and nearly died two years ago.

We finally reach the staircase and climb it, pulling ourselves out of the freezing water, only to find the door at the top to be locked.

Father puts me down, and Mother pulls me to her and wraps her arms around me.

Together, we watch as Father crashes once, twice, three times into the wooden door. He is grunting and shouting with each impact, and for what feels like the longest time, we all stand there watching him.

"Hurry," I hear Alice's voice whimpering behind me.

Mother, William and I turn to follow her gaze.

The water is climbing higher and higher up the staircase, one step at a time, like a monster slowly cornering us, and Alice takes a step back.

"Hurry, Father," I echo, my bottom lip trembling. I wipe my nose on my sleeve, suppress a sob.

Father inhales deeply, puffs it out, his gaze hyper focused on the door blocking our escape. And then, he releases one great, guttural scream and bashes his big shoulder into the door, and by some miracle, bursts through it.

Victor

By now, the Titanic was at such a tilt, there was no other option but to race uphill. With a steady pace, I move past crying children, screaming women, screaming men, and the imminent sound of the water sloshing all around us.

I climb over a railing, all decorum forgotten, and before I jump down to the lower deck, I look up to assess my surroundings.

The water is lapping up the forward promenade of B-deck like a slow slithering snake, like an ooze that would not be satisfied until it has consumed us all.

Everyone who is not already in a lifeboat – or has not already fallen into the water – is heading this way, a great wave of people with the same idea as me.

I am frozen for a moment, frozen in shock with the sight of it all – the chaos, the fear, the unknown.

Everyone looks the same, I realise, as they race towards me in their state of distress. I cannot discern any of my fellow nobles, nor can I easily pinpoint someone from steerage, those deemed *less than*.

With their white life vests on, their faces red and wet from screaming and crying, their hair in disarray, we are all the same. All of us desperate to survive, desperate to escape.

I jump down without much caution, collapse into a heap on the lower deck, get up, keep running.

I reach the other side of the ship, where more lifeboats are being filled, more distress rockets are being launched into the dark sky.

Suddenly I see Colonel Astor and his pregnant wife, Madeleine. He is helping her onboard one of the lifeboats, Madeleine gingerly holding her baby bump with one hand, as though she might otherwise lose it.

"John!" I call, and he turns to the sound.

"Victor," he replies as I approach, "are they allowing men on, on the other side?"

He knows the answer to that. Would I be here if they were?

But I shake my head, confirming what he already presumed.

"Blast!" he exclaims.

A rocket is released right next to us, and we both flinch at the sudden sound.

"We must make our way to the stern," I tell him.

He nods at me but does not move, turning instead to look at Madeleine as she makes herself comfortable.

I follow his gaze and remember suddenly their reason for this trip: to return home and get John's affairs in order, so that Madeleine and their child would be cared for if the worst were to happen to John.

Who would have thought that The Worst would come for them before they'd manage to outwit it?

I turn, look around. The water is rising quickly.

"We need to move, John," I tell him.

He completely ignores me this time, continuing only to stare at Madeleine, his moustache pulling down at the sides as his entire face droops in mourning.

I look about again, then back to John, before realising he will not move, and I could no longer wait for him to come to his senses.

With one final sigh, I shift past him, leaving behind the very man I had just last night hoped to befriend.

01:43

Ethel

Shortly after the shots were fired to keep people from storming the lifeboat, it was lowered with what looked to be just half capacity.

If they were filling them up properly, men would surely be allowed on by now!

The next boat is readied, and this time, Edward pushes me forward.

"Go," he says, and his voice is harder than I've ever heard it. I turn to him, but do not dare reply, the look in his eyes is so forceful.

Instead, I go forward as he commanded me, moving through the crowd of men. But I maintain my grip on his hand, dig my nails into his skin.

If I am going, then so is he.

We reach the boat – lifeboat 13 – but I hang back just for a moment.

There are already twenty people aboard, two officers helping a woman and her child over the threshold.

And this is when I take my chance.

I move quickly, lifting my skirts high for best mobility, then plop down beside a crying woman – and all the while I had dragged Edward with me.

To his credit, he did not protest, nor did he push back or try to let go when I pulled him onboard.

We sit there, among the women and children, none of them paying us any attention. I risk a glance at the officers, and neither of them has spotted Edward in the commotion.

I grab a blanket from beneath my seat and fling it over Edward's shoulders and head. He grabs the ends and holds them under his chin, hiding his face in shadow. He looks at me with wide eyes, stunned by his own actions, stunned by my conviction to stay together, whatever the cost. I meet his gaze for the briefest moment, communicating to him that this was the right thing to do. Man or not, we all deserved to survive this! No one, regardless of their sex, should be left behind because of the White Star Line's failure to adequately prepare in case of emergency. And I refused to lose my husband now, when he had only *just* returned to me.

I take another blanket and cover our knees.

We are now, at quick glance, no more than two shivering women, praying to come out of this nightmare alive.

"There's still room!" the officers shout into the crowd then, "There's room for more!"

And then, to our surprise, we look up to find another man climbing onboard, and another, and another.

"They're allowing men on board," I whisper bewilderedly to Edward, my heart briefly leaping with joy to know that, even if discovered, Edward would not be thrown off this lifeboat.

Then, in a wave of relief, distress and terror, I lean over the side and vomit into the abyss below.

Thomas

The guilt has found me. Guilt for having failed all these men, women and children.

I helped to build her, this *unsinkable* beast. This monstrous metal deathtrap.

My eyes sting, tears of shame to think that, had I just done a better job – had we *all* done a better job – none of this would be happening.

Then I think of Captain Smith, and how he received *six* iceberg warnings. *Six!*

I knew we should have slowed down. But did I question my superiors? No. I did what was expected of me, what I was paid for: to do my job and to do so without complaint.

The engine room is flooded. Many of my colleagues are already dead.

Not drowned as we feared but scalded to death by the steam when pipes broke away from the boilers, or crushed by the very machinery they have been trained to maintain.

They died doing their duty.

But it didn't make it any less horrifying.

Those of us hanging on continue at our posts, anything to keep the ship from plunging into total darkness.

I know death is close, I can hear it approaching with every hiss of steam, every burst of metal, every creak and groan of the ship as the bow trims more and more.

I inhale deeply, keep the tears at bay, and allow my boy's faces to fill my mind.

I hope they do not dwell on this, my untimely death. I hope that they are young enough to recover, to forget. I pray that at least William is…

William, my rambunctious five-year-old. I thanked God for his smile – the carbon copy of Jennie's – when she had died. Through his joy, I had retained some of my beloved wife, and even in my grief I had been thankful to have had a small piece of her left behind in him.

Thomas, my firstborn, my namesake, my best bud. He will take my abandonment to heart, will likely hate me for it; at least for a while. And I don't blame him; in fact, I hope he holds onto the anger for as long as he can. For anger is not as soul-consuming as pain, not as hazardous to the soul as sorrow.

I clench my teeth as the misery of their loss engulfs me, as the realisation that I will never see them again devours me.

I finally allow myself to expel my devastation, and I open my mouth to release a ghastly wail until my air is spent.

I cry as I continue to maintain the generator, my eyes squeezed shut to the horror that surrounds me.

At the peak of my doom, a light suddenly bursts through the darkness, and an apparition floats towards me.

I blink, my mouth hanging agog at the sight. The silhouette approaches slowly, the light behind it rendering its face in shadow.

Beside me, I'm vaguely aware of the sound of metal scraping, as though it's being torn away by a giant's hand.

And just as the angel stands before me and smiles – William's smile, *Jennie's* smile – I realise that this is the end.

The angel reaches one white hand towards me, as the sound all around me grows louder.

I tentatively extend my shivering hand, to take hers and escape this hell. And just as our fingertips brush, I hear Jennie's voice

in my ear, that gentle laugh I so adored. It fills me with such
bliss that, when the engine falls on top of me, crushing my body
in an instant, I do not feel any pain.
Only relief.

Michel

Over the megaphone, I hear Captain Smith ordering the lifeboats to return to the starboard side to pick up more passengers.

Maybe there was hope yet.

As the water reached higher and the ship inclined further, I took both my boys in my arms and hurried along the promenade, hopeful that maybe up here, the officers were allowing men to board the lifeboats.

"WOMEN AND CHILDREN!" one of them shouts into the crowd as I approach, and my heart sinks.

By now, most of the lifeboats are gone, the crew having uncovered the emergency, collapsible boats, and one of them is being filled right before me.

My whole body is shaking now. Whether from cold, fear, or sudden understanding, I do not know.

But it hits me then that I can no longer delay putting my kids on one of those boats.

I plop my sons down, and with a bended knee I hold them before me, one in each arm, holding them steady.

"Listen to me," I tell them, trying – and failing – to keep my voice from cracking.

"Papa?" Edmond squeaks, and my chest gives out.

I swallow my devastation.

"*Mes chéris,*" I say, then blow out my breath in quick succession, hoping to calm my nerves a little, "You must be brave for papa now."

Master grasps one of my fingers with his little hand, squeezes tightly. I look down at his hand, then up at his beautiful face.

"You must do this for me now. You will go in that lifeboat, take a seat, hold each other closely, and not stand up. You will be good boys, listen to the gentleman there," and I point to a crew member standing up in the collapsible lifeboat.

The boys follow where I am pointing, then turn back to me.

"He will take care of you until help arrives."

"And you?" Edmond asks now, "Will you come with us?"

I shake my head, pull them into a fierce embrace, "No, boys, I cannot come."

A scream from behind me snaps me out of my sorrow, brings me back to what I must do.

I stand, take my boys by each hand and head toward the lifeboat.

"Please," I call to the officer, "My sons."

He nods and picks up Master, heaves him into the boat as I do the same with Edmond.

"Their mother?" the officer asks me, and I merely shake my head.

He looks at me sheepishly, then nods, and for a moment I think he will let me on. But then he places a hand on my chest and keeps me from boarding.

I guide the boys to sit down, pointing to the bench. I bring a smile to my face to show them that all is well.

The officer's hand presses me backwards, and I do as I'm told. But I don't take my eyes off my children, both of which are staring blankly at me.

For a moment, I'm devastated they are not crying at our separation, but I quickly realise this is exactly what I wanted, what I needed: for them to think nothing of it, for them to think

I would follow on the next boat, or at least that they were not scared.

They look confused. But not frightened. And I know I did the best I could in this awful situation.

My heart pinches with guilt that I ever brought them here, that I ever thought stealing them from their mother would be a good idea. I suddenly realise that all the anger I felt towards my wife before now was just fear, distilled to its purest form.

Fear of losing her. Fear of a life without her.

But…wasn't I already living it?

I kidnapped my own sons. That's the truth of it.

And I, unintentionally, put them in harm's way.

But was it unintentional?

Even if this catastrophe had never happened, I had knowingly and wilfully taken them from their mother. That in itself was harmful to two young children, was it not?

But the reality of *why* I did what I did remains a mystery. At least to my wife – my ex-wife – who will never know the extent of my desperation to get her back, to fix our family, to mend the broken pieces of my life.

As the lifeboat containing my children and twenty other people begins to lower, a sudden need to absolve some of my guilt overcomes me, and I spring forward.

The officer's hand hovers over the hilt of his gun, worried for a moment that I would attempt to throw myself onto the lifeboat. But I am completely uncaring at this point. Let him shoot me. As long as I get to speak my truth.

I cup my hands at either side of my mouth and call Master. His little face, and Edmond's, snap up and they find me. I take a mental snapshot of the image before me: the last time I will ever see them.

"My children!" I call, "when your mother comes for you, as she surely will, tell her that I loved her dearly and still do. Tell her that I hoped she would follow us. Tell her…that I am sorry." Master nods, lifts his little hand and waves at me, his expression blank.

An old lady sitting beside them realises they are onboard unsupervised and shifts closer to them. I watch as she pulls a blanket out from underneath her and wraps it around both my boys, and I silently thank her for doing what I cannot.

Mon copies his older brother then, lifting his own pudgy hand to wave at me, and he gifts me a bright smile. The old lady follows his gaze and, with tears in her eyes, nods once at me. I know what she is trying to convey.

I smile back at them, blow my boys one last kiss, and nod to the woman in thanks. And when the lifeboat hits the water, I turn away, hating myself for having failed my children so miserably.

Catherine

We escaped the knee-high water only briefly upon bursting through the door, a great gush of it meeting us as soon as we fled through into the hallway.

It all happened so fast.

One minute Alice was behind us, and in the next breath she was gone…

I didn't even hear her scream. None of us did.

We don't linger, we can't afford to.

Mother is holding onto my hand as she drags me along now, her fingers in a death grip to keep me from being swept away.

William is on Father's back, piggy-backing like we used to when we were little.

And as I watch my nine-year-old brother hanging onto Father's back like an overgrown monkey, a cold finger of understanding brushes over my spine.

We may yet be trapped in the bodies of small, young children, but William and I have grown up in the space of a heartbeat the second we were roused from sleep tonight.

I think of the conversation I had with Alice just yesterday – my throat closing with fresh tears to think of her, floating dead somewhere in these halls – and of how she advised me not to grow up.

I understand it now.

Being a child meant you could think to others to keep you safe.

Being a grown up meant knowing that nothing – not even those who love you more than life itself – could keep you safe from certain dangers.

As we turn another corner, my mother dragging me behind her, I feel my hand slipping from hers. The water around my waist is freezing – like a thousand tiny knives digging into my skin – and it is unrelenting.

And, somehow, I know that I will not make it to a lifeboat, that likely…none of us will.

"Hold on, baby!" Mother shouts as she tries to grab me with her other hand.

By this point, the water has swept me up off the floor, my feet no longer able to keep me where I want to be.

A scream escapes me, followed by William's voice as he calls my name in sheer panic.

The ship moans and *ticks* all around us, water spurting in even from small tears in the steel ceiling.

I look up to see the faces of my family staring wide-eyed at me, then around themselves as they realise that I am not the only one to worry about.

My hand slips from Mother's then as a shriek escapes me and I am sucked down the hallway, my family's screams following me, my own scream echoing above the loud whirlpools surrounding us.

I fling my arms around in the icy water, as though I could swim back. I grab onto the corner of the hallway we had just come from. Or was it the one we had been trying to reach?

I don't know anymore. And it no longer matters.

My head comes out the top of the water and I breathe in a deep breath and open my eyes. I can just about see them, their heads bobbing near the ceiling, too high for them to be simply standing...

I can hear my mother crying hysterically, my father pleading with her to keep going. But then they, too, are pushed under the seawater.

"Mummy!" is all I'm able to scream before the water engulfs me just moments after seeing my family be taken.

The salt stings my eyes and burns my throat, and as I'm whirled around and around, bashed into the wall, the ceiling, the floor, my lungs burn as I inhale the seawater, I do not think about the pain, or what we might find after death. All I can think about in my final moments of consciousness, is how I wished I'd never stopped calling her 'Mummy'.

Victor

Shots are fired into the air.

I don't know from which direction they came, the screams and cries all around me diluting any other sound.

I continue ahead, manoeuvring past people – some young, some old, some women…mostly men.

I hear another gunshot, and this time my head snaps around, identifying its location. I don't know why I looked, perhaps to ascertain that I was not hit? Perhaps because curiosity is part of our human nature?

No one is hurt – not for the gun anyway – but in my wonder I notice a lifeboat – perhaps the final one – being lowered, and a man climbing on.

With my mouth hanging open in disbelief, I hurry towards it, sure that I am saved and that *finally* men were allowed to board.

"Is there room? Is there more room?"

My voice does not sound like my own, so desperate, so fraught. I crane my neck to take in the sight: one of the emergency collapsible lifeboats, filled almost to capacity with women and children, and one lone man. I recognise him. I have seen him before. Bruce Ismay is the only man among them.

A hand grips my upper arm then and swivels me around, the officer with the gun pointing it at me and shouting at me to GET BACK!

"But, Mr Ismay –" I lurch forward slightly, my arm outstretched to pinpoint the man hiding among the women.

The officer forces me back, "Get back, sir!" he shouts again, his face beetroot red, his eyes wide and wild.

I open my mouth to protest when suddenly a loud *bang* bursts through the night, cancelling out all other sound.

A wisp of smoke swirls lazily between us, almost obscuring my view of the officer's shocked expression.

He is looking down at my middle, and I, confused, follow his gaze.

So strange.

I hadn't *felt* the bullet going in. And yet it must have, because I am bleeding profusely from my gut.

Automatically, I press my hand to the hole in my belly, as though to conceal it from view would erase its existence.

Completely involuntarily, I fall to my knees, my mouth working open and closed, trying to expel my confusion.

And then I collapse, face first, onto the wooden decking, my final thought in this life being that I should have known better than to argue through the chaos with common sense.

For *of course*, Bruce Ismay would have been allowed to flee on a lifeboat. After all, he was the White Star Line director.

02:10

Ethel

We were fools to think that getting on a lifeboat meant we were safe!

Just moments after we'd felt the boat smack into the black water below and bob its way along, screams erupted all around us.

Edward and I looked up and immediately my stomach sank to see the bottom of another lifeboat coming down directly over our heads.

"Stop! Stop!" I heard myself scream as the other women, children and men hollered similar warnings. Some of the men stood up and tried to keep the other craft from descending as the women cowered down, all of us hunched over or with our arms around the little ones aboard.

Luckily, the officers must have heard us, or maybe the men were able to push us along quicker by pressing off the other lifeboat with their bare hands, but suddenly we were no longer in harm's way, our boat floating out from underneath just as the other descended where we had just been.

Immediately, people grabbed the oars and started moving away from the ship and its other deadly lifeboats, into – what we hoped would finally be – safety.

That was half an hour ago, and none of us has breathed a word since.

From our position about a mile away from the Titanic, we have the mortifying privilege of witnessing its horrific descent into darkness.

The anguished cries of those onboard is like one great human wail. And I am certain the sound will haunt me forever.

From where we bob in the protection of our lifeboat, we can clearly see the slow incline of the great ship as the water consumes it at the bow. It has almost reached the collapsibles on the boat deck, and I feel sick to think of how many lives are still onboard.

"We need to go back," I hear myself whisper, a cloud of white fog bursting out of me, like dragon's breath.

No one replies, but I know they are all thinking the same thing: If we go back now, it is likely that the frantic people in the water will pull us in with them in their haste to climb aboard.

And the reality that we would have to wait and observe the ship disappear underwater completely before we could safely aid the others, made the hairs on the back of my neck stand up.

Soon, we would be drifting on water which possessed dozens – nay, *hundreds* – of dead people. Men, women, and children. Frozen to death, or drowned, or their bodies broken from their fall into the water...I shudder to think of it, my stomach twisting into a knot.

The Titanic's sudden loud groan forces my eyes to it yet again, as though demanding my attention.

I don't want to look. I don't want to see this.

But it's the least I can do – as I sit here with my own life ahead of me – to give those who are dying right before my eyes the acknowledgement they deserve.

Many will be forgotten, especially those in third class, their bodies likely never to be recovered. And if they are, they will probably be so spoiled they will be unidentifiable.

I press my lips together tightly, grip my frozen hand underneath the thin blanket, and raise my eyes to the disaster.

All these people deserve our undivided attention now. All of them.

So, I make myself watch their final moments as if my own life depends on it.

It is the very least I can do, to try to remember those who will this night be lost forever.

Michel

I watch in horror as the onyx water reaches one of the ship's massive funnels, its cords snapping one by one, and the giant metal tube falling on top of dozens of people swimming for their lives in the open sea.

The sound the funnel makes on impact with the water – and the bodies within it – is unlike anything I have ever heard.

Its weight as it descends below creates a giant suction hole, taking many nearby people under with it, their screams sliced in half as they are pulled into the abyss.

Tears sting my eyes, and I'm ashamed to say it is not tears of sorrow for those unlucky bastards, but of fear for my own life.

My bladder has already failed me, and now so do my thoughts.

I am scared.

I am *terrified*.

I am certain I am no longer in my right mind.

And I am just glad that I held onto my senses long enough to see my sons to safety.

I would never forgive myself if they had seen their papa in this pathetic state.

Not only for the preservation of my already tainted memory, but also for the fact that it would have caused them much distress.

I may have been a flawed husband, a less than perfect friend, a mediocre businessman. But I was a *good* father! No matter what the authorities said when they took them into temporary care when Marcelle and I separated...

And I would take that truth with me, let it warm me in this storm. I would keep it safe in my pocket like a memento, until my final breath.

I am already at the stern, where everyone has been fleeing towards. From this position, holding on tightly to the railings, I bear witness to an incredible sight. Though I'd never wished to see it, I cannot deny that it is extraordinary.

With the water now reaching the base of the second funnel, the ship begins to tip further, causing the stern to rise rapidly and the propellers to emerge from under the dark water.

I cannot help but look down as I hang onto the railing.

They are *impressive*!

Many people jump into the water now, no doubt terrified into action before they think it through. I watch three, four, five people dive in from this great height, knowing all of them will die upon impact with the icy ocean below. One of them misjudges their jump and their head smacks into the propeller on their way down. That lucky sod will, at least, be dead before they even reach the water.

But maybe they weren't as impulsive as I initially thought.

After all, I too do not intend to drown today.

I tap my breast pocket to make sure it is still there, and sigh with relief at the feel of it.

I look around one more time, clasp on as the ship's stern continues to rise, as those around me scream, many falling as they fail to hold on.

I extend my gaze to the waves beyond, hoping to catch one last glimpse of Master and Edmond.

Again, my mind breaking…

Of course I will not see them. Not only are they likely miles away, but the sea around us is as black as the ace of spades. I couldn't see anything no matter how hard I tried.

With that knowledge – and as the ship threatens to lurch underneath me – I unlatch one of my hands from the railing and slowly bring it to my breast pocket.

I am mildly impressed with myself that my hand is not shaking. Perhaps I really am glad for it to end this way.

I retrieve my revolver from my jacket and hold it firmly in my steady hand.

Then, very carefully, I straighten my back and lift my face to the heavens as I bring the revolver to my temple.

I shiver at the gun's cold kiss against my skin.

I will drink in one last beautiful view, the twinkling stars above us being clearer than I have ever seen them. And I realise that, with my death – and that of everyone else onboard – the world will keep on spinning.

I take comfort in that knowledge – that my sons' world will not stop because of my demise. It is a blissful thought to focus on in this final moment.

I thank God for my life, one rich with love, ambition and success. I thank God that I had my sons when I did, so that they are young enough yet to perhaps not even remember this fateful night.

I mull over that hope. Turn it into a prayer.

And with one slow exhale, I pull the trigger.

02:18

Ethel

I hear another gunshot, but by now it is not so unexpected. But I also see the spark that came from its release, and my eyes instinctively zero in on the horrific scene of a man falling down the length of the tilting ship, his limp limbs smacking against a giant propeller before he hits the water.

I swallow my nausea and wonder how terrified of drowning he must have been to take his own life.

I wonder who it might have been, if we'd met him on the ship. I wonder if he had a family. If they are safe, and why he did not board a lifeboat as Edward and the handful of other men here did.

Were we the only lifeboat that allowed men?

I shudder to think of it. Surely not…

But I cannot spare much thought on that one particular horror, as so much more unfolds before me.

A giant roar bursts through the night as the Titanic snaps in half suddenly, and a collective scream vibrates off the top of the sea towards us. The distress in their voices is deafening, and many of us in the lifeboat gasp in alarm at the sight.

One half of the ship is pulled under, taking the other half with it quickly. Titanic stands with her stern raised high then, and everything not nailed down plummets into the ocean.

Deck chairs, tables…people…

Then…it just stands there…for what feels like an age.

"What's happening?" I whisper, and Edward takes my hand as he, too, stares wide-eyed at the scene before us.

Fifteen seconds pass. Then twenty. And the whole time we hold our breath, the only sound now being that of the people splashing about in the water around the ship.

Finally, her stern begins to descend again, creating a suction, churning the water around it and taking with it anyone too close.

There is a person standing at the top of it, riding it down like an elevator. He jumps off at the last minute.

And then, the unsinkable Titanic and countless lives are gone.

04:00

Edward

When I returned from New York to England to marry Ethel Clarke, I had promised to keep her safe.

Unbeknownst to me – or anyone – by boarding the Titanic, I had already failed in keeping that promise just four days after our small wedding.

Growing up with nine siblings meant I had seen – and participated in – my fair share of fights. My three older brothers used to love a good punch up. My sisters' boyfriends were, more often than not, a bad egg which my brothers and I would happily pay a visit to when they mistreated them.

I've had broken bones more often than I care to remember, ranging from the standard bust-up nose to the fractured tibia. I've even had my eye socket broken. I can still feel the indent of it if I press under my eye.

But despite all that – or perhaps because of it – I thought myself invincible in my twenties, as though nothing would ever hurt me.

I hadn't been in a proper brawl for years now though, not really. Ever since I proposed to Ethel and vowed to be worthy of her, I had kept my head down and done little else but work. So that we would be able to build a life together in America.

But that belief was still very much within me, the belief that I was invincible. I guess because I'd never had reason to believe otherwise.

And then the Titanic struck an iceberg, and I saw the world as I knew it descend into hell, narrowly dragging me and Ethel down with it.

I will admit, I have never been so frightened in my entire life!

Not when Sam Ryan pulled a knife on me.

Not when I got beaten to a pulp by a group of lads who jumped me one night after I beat their buddy at billiard.

Not when my brother got hit by a car right in front of me.

Those moments had all scared me, all on their own scale.

But what happened tonight? That kind of fear, I'm sure, will never leave me.

And neither, I think, will the guilt.

I may have survived the sinking – one of only a few men – but the ordeal has already changed me, as surely as a disease infects its host. As a man, I was meant to stay behind…

We have not even been rescued yet, and already I can feel the remorse eating away at me.

"Edward?"

I hear my beautiful wife's voice beside me, no more than a whisper, and I open my eyes.

I try to, anyway.

They feel like they are glued shut, my – and everyone's – eyelashes having frozen in the cold.

I pry my lids apart, blink away the pain, and find comfort in the sight of my wife's face.

I smile up at her. At least I think I do, my face is so cold, I cannot feel anything besides the skin cracking with the effort.

Ethel breathes a sigh of relief at my show of life, and the mist of her breath encircles me.

I realise I am lying down, so I try to sit up, to give her some comfort. It is a struggle, and I am only able to do so because Ethel has grabbed one of my frozen hands and is pulling me to her.

It has gone quiet.

The splashing, screaming, and crying has diminished entirely. Have they already been saved?

"How long was I asleep?" I ask her. My voice is raspy. I wrap one arm around her, hoping to share our body heat under the ice-crusted blanket on our knees.

"I don't know," she whispers, looking out into the black ocean, "the sky has not yet broken, no dawn in sight. Perhaps an hour?"

I nod my head slowly, realising what the unnerving silence truly means.

I rub my hand up and down her arm, and notice she is clutching something.

"What's this?" I ask.

She looks down at her arms, as though she's forgotten she was holding it, "Oh," she says, blinking like she's in a dream, "I saw it floating by our boat – earlier."

She turns it around to show me. It's a book. A completely sodden, unsavable book.

I frown at her, and she looks down at it, "The Secret Garden," she mumbles numbly.

I don't know why she chose to pluck this particular item out of the sea, but I do not question it. Instead, I press a kiss to her freezing cold forehead.

"Help will be with us soon," I tell her, "I know it."

She turns her red-cheeked face to me. Her nose is dripping, her lips are cracked, and her eyelashes are like tiny snow-covered pine trees. And still she is the loveliest thing I have ever seen.

But she looks at me in fear, in worry, and I hate that I cannot give her any more assurance.

And then, just as my throat was tightening with the possibility of death despite our escape, we hear the sweet sound of a horn. And we all gasp or sob with alleviation.

Master

I'm cold, and Edmond keeps leaning over the side to touch the water.

A man is sitting next to him to keep him from falling in.

The old lady who was next to me has gone to sleep. She's been asleep a while. I wonder if I should poke her cheek like I sometimes do to papa when he's snoring.

But the old lady isn't snoring, so I guess I'll leave her alone.

She's not doing much of anything really. I don't think she's even moved since that man came to sit next to Edmond.

The man says something now, but I don't know what he's saying. He is speaking funny.

He waves a biscuit at me and I take it eagerly, stuffing it in my mouth. As I'm chewing, he smiles at me, and I wonder why he is here when my papa isn't. I wonder where papa went after he put us in this little boat. If he had to go into a different little boat.

"Master?" Edmond says then. His teeth are chattering, and I scooch closer to him.

"Where's papa?" he asks me.

I shrug and look up at the man sitting next to us, as if he might know.

He catches my eye and looks about the boat with a sad expression. Then he licks his lips and puts on that smile again.

"Hugh," he says, pressing the palm of his hand against his chest, then he points at me and Edmond.

I frown. I think he wants to know our names.

Edmond opens his mouth to answer then, when I remember papa has special names for us on this trip, "John," I say, interrupting my little brother. Then I point at Edmond beside me, "Fred."

Edmond looks at me and then giggles, "*Oui*, Fred," he says in confirmation, stabbing his fat thumb into his chest.

The man – Hugh? – nods at us. Then he offers us another biscuit each, almost like a reward for a question well answered; and as we eat them, I notice someone leaning over the old lady next to me.

I don't know what it means when they touch her wrist, or when they look up at the officer and shake their head.

But I do know that I want another biscuit, so I decide to stay close to Hugh.

Maria

I'm rocking back and forth like a madwoman. I know I must look like one.

And yet I do not care.

With the icy blanket around my shoulders and our collective exhales causing a pathetic little fog before us, my frantic rocking is the only thing keeping me warm – and, ironically, sane.

There are two men on our lifeboat. Both threw themselves on from the second-class deck as it was being lowered. One of them broke his leg, I am sure, the crack of his fall was so loud. And I only wish Victor had been so cavalier.

Victor is surely dead, I know it. I can feel it in my heart.

He said he would buy his way onto a boat. But somehow, I am not sure that his money has saved him.

A noise escapes my throat and my stomach clenches with sorrow.

Victor could be a *burro* – an ass – but he was *my burro!* And I loved him more than I could ever describe.

Loved…

Are we already thinking of our men in the past tense? Are any other of these women having the same thought?

I look around at them, some look my age, some are old. And I think how absolutely tragic it must be to live your life with your best friend, to grow old and frail, and then to be separated so disturbingly. These old women's husbands have little chance of surviving this icy water.

And it gives me a pinch of comfort to think that Victor, at least, was young, he was fit, he was healthy…Perhaps there is hope for him yet.

But do I dare to hope? When it is such a fragile thing? Like a baby bird in the palm of your hand?

"*Dona,*" Mina's voice comes to me now, sparing me from my inner turmoil.

I grace her with my full attention, but she is craning her neck, looking wide-eyed into the nothingness.

"*Creo que veo un barco.*"

Immediately, I am upright. So swiftly that the entire lifeboat rocks, and several of the women exclaim in fright.

"A ship?" I say, "You see a ship?"

Mina pulls me back down, then points her finger into the distance, "*Creo que si.*"

By now, the officer and the women and children are looking into the darkness where Mina is pointing. The officer's torch illuminates a small circle beyond us, and I squint around it.

"Turn it off," I tell him after a moment.

"What?" he replies. No manners.

"Turn it *off!*" I repeat, waving my frosted hand at him.

He does as I say, and we all hold our breath as we search the night.

"There!" one of the women croaks, "Right there, I see lights!"

Like a group of hens, we all begin to agree, some of us laughing with relief, others crying for the same reason.

We are saved. But are our men?

04:45

Edward

    White gulls call.

And we can finally make out the horizon. Across the sea a pale sun rises, and with it, a ship has come to carry us home.

The sky has turned from pitch black to a dim lilac by the time Ethel and I are rescued from our lifeboat.

The ship is called the Carpathia, and though it's wildly less grand than the Titanic, the wonderful sight of her will forever live on in my mind's eye.

Many of my fellow passengers, including myself – much to my embarrassment – were in an unfit state to climb to safety; and so, as our craft nudged against Carpathia's hull, we were one-by-one gradually lifted, with either bosun's chairs or canvas bags, onto the ship.

Ethel and I were one of the first to be plucked from lifeboat 13, and we now sit on two deckchairs on the boat deck, wrapped in fresh blankets, and with a steaming, hot beverage in our hands. We sit in silence as we sip our drinks and observe the slow and steady stream of survivors filling the deck over the lip of our mugs.

As just a few hours earlier while we were patiently waiting for the lifeboats to be prepared on the Titanic – before the chaos truly erupted – everyone climbing onto the Carpathia is strangely silent. Though none of us are calm.

I am still shaking, despite having thawed my exterior. And I know it's due to nerves.

I cannot think to face the officer that is approaching to ask us questions, to take our statement.

What will I tell the world?!

Will I tell them that I was pulled onto the lifeboat by my wife? That a woman forced me to claim my God given right to save myself?

What of all those other poor fellows who did not get the chance to force their way on?

We were instructed: Women and children *first*.

And I…I took one of those spaces meant for one of those women…one of those children.

I know that not all the women and children were evacuated in time, we all saw several of them still running up the inclining boat deck to the stern as it sank, some holding newborns in their arms…some dragging toddlers behind them.

My stomach clenches at the disturbing image flashing in my mind like a burst of lightning, and I lean forward, sure I am about to be sick. But I stop myself, force it down.

"Edward?" Ethel says from beside me.

I can feel her gentle hand on my back, rubbing it lovingly. But it does nothing to alleviate my nausea. My guilt.

I know she means well, but it feels like her hand is burning a hole in my clothes, searing my skin, and I brush her off.

"I'm alright," I tell her, though I feel anything but.

I press my thumb and forefinger into my eyes, squeeze them shut to block out the memories of the bodies floating in the dark water around us as we awaited our saviours.

Someone clears their throat, and I slowly look up.

"Name?"

The young man standing before me must be no more than in his mid-thirties – the same age as me – but somehow, I feel decades older.

He looks down at me and Ethel with a clipboard in one hand and a pencil in another.

"Beane," I tell him as I straighten my back, hold onto my last shred of dignity, "Edward and Ethel Beane."

He takes note.

The acid in my stomach is lurching.

"Mr and Mrs Beane," the young officer says, "Do you wish to give your account?"

I look at Ethel, who presses her lips together briefly, as though attempting a smile. Or suppress a sob. I cannot tell.

I nod slowly at the man, inhale. And then, to spare my guilty conscience, I lie.

07:00

The wind eventually picked up and waves buffeted our little lifeboat so much that I was certain for a moment we would capsize before we could reach the Carpathia.

But eventually we did, the sun shining over the horizon now brightening the path ahead.

The man with the broken leg – which I can now see has a piece of bone sticking clean out – is carefully lifted up first, then the women and children, and lastly the other man and the officer.

I am a block of ice by the time I am transferred from the lifeboat to the more solid deck of the Carpathia and all I want to do is lay down my weary head.

Mina and I, along with a couple other women from our boat, are ushered up to the higher deck, separating us first-class survivors from steerage.

And it's the first time in hours that I've considered myself and those women to be separate creatures.

It appears not even a disaster such as this can unify us for very long. All it took was for the rigid social structure we humans have created to, yet again, make our differences abundantly clear.

Mina and I are made comfortable and offered a glass of whiskey or brandy or scotch. I do not care what it is.

Mina asks for a cup of coffee, but I need to dull my senses and I gladly accept whatever liquor they have to offer.

I sit back then, my legs bent underneath me, the blanket wrapped tightly around me, and with my glass of gold liquid in my hands as I watch the lifeboats coming in, one by one.

Across the horizon I can see the dozens of icebergs all around us. Some are small, but some are quite vast and wide and despite the liquor warming my insides, the clear sight of them sends a shiver down my spine.

As the sun rises higher, the darkness of the sea turns to silver glass, its light on the water shimmering as though nothing at all has happened last night.

With each lifeboat that is rescued without a sign of Victor, my hope begins to fade, and the reality that we have come to our end clasps its barbed hooks around my heart. And squeezes.

07:10

Master

Edmond and I were the first to be moved from our little boat onto the bigger boat, holding onto each other as we were put in a burlap sack and hoisted up.

Edmond giggled all the way up.

I searched the big water for papa.

As we are plucked from the burlap sack by two strangers, I think, *This is it. Now we will finally see mama again. We will find papa.*

But instead, a man takes us by the hand and walks us past so many people. Some are sitting on the floor, some are pacing up and down, some are standing and staring into the distance. Most of them are crying.

He takes us to a deck chair – one of the few that is still free – where he sits us down and throws a blanket over our legs, another around us, and deposits chocolates on our laps.

Edmond tucks into the treats, but I am more cautious. I don't want this man here. I don't want this chocolate. I want my mama and papa!

The man inhales now, unsure. Then he says, "John?"

I nod slowly, but then he continues in a language I do not know. I look to Edmond, who grins at me, his face covered in the brown, sweet treat.

I look down at my own chocolate and take a bite. And all the while, the man is still speaking.

"*Où est notre mère?*" I ask him when he finally stops, and I see his eyes grow wide.

Edmond jumps up then, "*Oui, oui! Mama, mama!*"

He is looking around excitedly, as if by mentioning her it will make our mama magically appear.

But papa *did* say that she would come find us…

The man looks over his shoulder now, then back at us with a smile on his face, but his eyes look worried. He lifts one finger and wags it at us before walking away, and I get the sense he wants us to stay put.

"Where is mama?" Edmond asks me again.

"I don't know," I reply, and my tummy flips at the thought that we may never see either of our parents ever again.

Edmond has fallen asleep next to me, his thumb in his mouth and a chocolate gripped in his other hand.

It's melting onto his jacket, and I think papa will not be pleased to see him so dirty.

All around us there are people weeping. Some of them, like Edmond, are asleep. But mostly…there is a lot of weeping.

I search the crowd for papa. Or mama. The face of *anyone* that I know.

But they are all strangers, and – after all this time – my eyes begin to sting with tears.

My chin is wobbling as I continue to look around. I can feel my chest going up and down quickly, and I'm trying not to wake Edmond with my fear, when suddenly I see the man from earlier returning with a woman in tow.

The man is saying something to her, but she hurries right past him and takes a seat on the edge of our deck chair.

"Hello, you two," she says to us in French.

I don't know this person. But finally understanding someone makes me feel calmer.

"*Bonjour*," I reply.

Edmond continues to sleep next to me.

"My name is Miss Hays," she tells me as she smiles, "You can call me Miss Hays, or you can call me Margaret. What's your name?"

Immediately, my chest feels heavy with the lie I think papa would want us to tell, but I say it anyway, for surely, he changed our names for our protection.

"I'm John, and that's Fred."

She nods at my response.

"And you are alone?"

I look around for good measure, then, "Yes. Papa put us on the little boat. He said mama would come get us."

"And your mama, have you seen her here?"

I shake my head, "Our mama was not with us."

"On the lifeboat?"

"On the big boat."

"The Titanic?"

I nod, "Papa said she would come later."

"Ah," Miss Hays says, then nods at the officer behind her. She tells him something in the language I don't understand, and when he walks away, she turns back to us.

"I will stay here with you for a while, *d'accord*?" she says, "Until we find your mama."

I cannot help the grin that splits my face, I am so grateful.

"You will help us find mama?"

She nods at me slowly, reaches over and cups my cheek.

"Of course, *cheri*, we will soon find out what is going on here."

1 MONTH LATER

Master

Nobody came to find us, and we ended up staying with Miss Hays while people looked for our mama and papa.

Miss Hays was very kind. She took care of us in her big house and made sure to always play with us during the day and read a bedtime story at night.

Edmond calls her Maggie, and he seems to like her very much. When we first got here, he would ask me and Miss Hays every day where our mama and papa are. I would look hopefully to Miss Hays, but she would always have the same answer.

I don't know.

Sometimes she would say, *We will find them.*

As the days went by, Edmond would ask less and less, and soon he stopped asking altogether.

Often, people would come to Miss Hays' house to take pictures of us, and to ask us questions. They call us the 'Titanic Orphans'. I don't know what that means.

We never knew how to answer their queries, even when Miss Hays would translate so that we could understand.

Some days ago, though, I heard Miss Hays speak with the men in the other room, and I was certain I had heard her murmuring our real names, *Master. Edmond.*

I thought back to the last few weeks in her home, wondered if I had slipped up and forgotten to address Edmond as Fred.

But nothing came to mind.

Edmond must have told her.

I became frantic, my breathing coming too quickly and tears stinging the back of my eyes.

Our secret was out. What would happen if papa found out?

But over the next few days, Miss Hays continued to call us John and Fred, and never once let on that she knew those were not actually our names.

Perhaps I had misheard.

Perhaps it was all a fantasy.

But now, as Edmond and I play with a wooden train set in the lounge, we hear a knock at the front door, followed by a voice that sounds familiar. As though I'd heard it once in a dream.

I stand up and Edmond watches me take a step towards the door to the hall, when suddenly quick and heavy footsteps sound, like someone is running towards us.

I gasp in fear and turn back. Edmond covers his face with his hands.

But then, we lay eyes on our mama, our beautiful, crying, smiling mama. And everything is right again in the world.

We are found.

Marcelle

I was young and naïve when I had agreed to marry Michel.
Don't get me wrong, I had loved him desperately. He and I
were, to begin with, very much in love.
But love blinds you to the less favourable characteristics of a
person, and you deliberately ignore them, maybe even believe
yourself to be the very cure to those behaviours.
I will fix him.
We married in London, though he was originally from Slovakia
and had emigrated to France, and I, Italian. The reason for this
may appear sinister, now that I have the beauty of hindsight.
But at the time I was so swept off my feet by love that I thought
nothing of it.
I was only seventeen when I married Michel, you see. And in
France, there was a law in place which did not allow for a
woman younger than twenty-two to marry without their
parents' or guardians' consent.
And we most certainly did not have my parents' consent.
But Michel figured out a plan. He found out that there was no
such law in England, and without further ado we made the trip
and were swiftly wed. Defying my parents felt good.
Liberating. Grown up.
I should have known they were trying to protect me.
But I trusted Michel in all things back then. After all, he was
the well-travelled, charismatic gentleman who seemed to know
the answer to everything.
We were happy for a while. I won't pretend and lie that we were
not. We were!

We had our two beautiful sons, Michel had – what I believed to have been – a thriving business. Things were looking good. Our future appeared without hiccups.

But I should have known that the less favourable side of Michel that I had glimpsed even as a green teenager, would come forth one day. And truthfully, I had been a fool to think myself his saviour all those years ago.

Love does not change a person.

It only blunts their sharp edges for as long as that love is more powerful than their other emotions.

His passion for me – as is natural, I am sure – faded over time, and before long, I was no more his beloved wife, but his personal servant.

He made me work, unpaid, from dawn until dusk each day. He often insulted me in front of the other workers, too, sometimes threatening me with violence. Other times he would ignore my presence entirely, behaving as though I didn't exist.

I cherished those days after a while, the lesser of two evils.

But then he began disappearing, sometimes for days on end, without telling me or his workers where he was going.

Some days he would leave without warning but return in the early hours of the morning.

But each time upon his return, he would scold me for a whore, insulting me in the most derogatory of ways, as if *I* were the one sneaking off at night or for days on end.

His jealousy was the most frightening of moods, for I didn't know what it would lead him to do.

He refused to sit with me and the boys at supper from then on, my poor sons having no understanding as to what they had done to deserve such rejection. But they were easily distracted, still young enough to forget a moment of sadness with a happy song or a game of hide and seek.

But I could not forget.

I felt abandoned. I felt lonely. I felt sad. But more often than not, I felt scared.

And then one day, without cause or warning, Michel threw a plate at me.

It didn't hit me – physical activity was never Michel's strong suit. In fact, he had told me very early on in our marriage that it shamed him to admit he could not even swim!

So the plate smashed into a thousand pieces on the parquet instead. He insulted me too, calling me 'a woman of the gutter', 'a fishwife', and 'a woman of no substance.'

Each insult felt like a blow to the gut.

Made even worse for the fact that our two little boys were observing the whole thing, frozen to the spot in fear.

And it was in that moment, and because of the look on their innocent faces, that I decided I would divorce my once wonderful husband.

In the months that followed, and before our divorce was finalised, I'll admit that I met someone. And I will admit that I committed adultery.

But by this point I was no longer married in my heart.

It's funny…Michel never had cause to be so grotesquely jealous while we were together. Now he did, however – at last he had an actual reason to hate me! And it was all due to his own doing.

Michel found out of course, and this did not look good for me during our court proceedings. He went on to use my one mistake against me, made me out to be a lustful slut, that I was sleeping with half of Nice! And they didn't know what to do with all that. *Both* parents now appeared unfit…

It got ugly for a time, so much so that the judge even ruled for our boys to be taken from us *both* for a while and put into temporary care until a more solid decision was made.

Those two weeks were the longest of my life.

I had wept day and night to be separated from my babies, and all because I allowed myself some happiness by taking another man to my bed!

I had been foolish. I had been selfish.

But soon the boys and I were reunited, the judge granting Michel and I shared custody.

I had thought all would be well from then on, had thought the worst was behind me.

For surely, what else could go wrong? What could *possibly* be worse?

As it turned out…so much.

I had dropped Edmond and Master off at their father's for the Easter holidays. Had squeezed them both tightly and kissed them each on the crowns of their heads before ushering them inside and reminding them to be good.

But when Michel failed to return them to me, my wild search began.

Who would have thought that Michel would go to such lengths to hurt me? I certainly never did.

He took them all over Europe, apparently, before buying tickets for the Titanic.

Master told me, some moments after our sweet reunion at that Miss Margaret Hays' residence, that their papa had a message for me. That he loved me and always had.

I had smiled at my two babies at the confession, had pressed them to me and squeezed so tightly that Edmond cried out and wriggled free.

I had pretended to be touched by their father's hypocritical message, then I'd thanked Miss Hays profusely for finding and looking after my babies, and I took them home.

They asked for their papa for a while longer, until they realised that I did not – or would not – give them much of an answer.

I had my reasons. And they weren't malicious. Not at all.

But how do you tell two little boys that their papa has died? That he would not ever come home?

He had been a bad husband, had done some terrible things, but the boys loved him fiercely. And from what I have gathered over the weeks that followed their return, he took excellent care of them during their excursion. They had – by all accounts – had the time of their lives.

And I wanted to shield them for as many years as possible of Michel's tragic demise.

When the time comes for them to find out that their papa had perished on the Titanic – one of the roughly 1500 who had not made it out alive – I will allow them to remain blissfully ignorant why they were there to begin with. To protect them from the fact that he had quite literally abducted them.

What would be the point of staining their final moments with him?

Edmond doesn't remember much, but Master tells me it was quite the adventure. There is never any fear or sadness or hurt in their fragmented stories, so I feel no need to sully their memory of him now that he is dead.

He had been a troubled man. Of that, I am sure.

But my sons would not grow up hearing terrible things about him. I would give the father of my children that much, at least.

After all, he has paid for his sins with his life.

And though I had hated him for many months, and despite everything he did, he had not deserved to die on that ship.

No matter a person's shortcomings, *no one* deserved such a terrible fate.

4 MONTHS LATER

Maria

We weren't even supposed to be on the Titanic!

Victor's mother had warned us after our wedding that no matter what, we must not set foot on a boat of any kind.

She had these strange premonitions sometimes, Victor had informed me, followed by that laugh of his. That laugh that I will never hear again.

We'd brushed it off as an old woman's ramblings and went off on our honeymoon, completely forgetting about it.

And when we saw posters for that damned ship, Victor and I just *couldn't* resist. We *couldn't*. Of course not! Because our wealth had made us believe nothing could touch us; that we *deserved* to be on that luxurious voyage.

Victor was so crafty, he even planned for his own servant to stay behind in Paris and to send his mother postcards while we were on the Titanic, so that she would be none the wiser as to our actual whereabouts.

But…if she is to be believed, she knew that Victor was dead even before *I* had fully accepted it yet. On the very day of its sinking, she had – apparently – had a fly land in her soup?

I wasn't really listening.

Point is, she was beside herself.

And that, at least, I could understand.

To make matters worse – was that even possible? – Victor's body had not been recovered. My father and I had even travelled down to Halifax to see if the Mackay-Bennet – the ship that recovered the majority of the bodies after the sinking – had found him.

I must admit, I had been hopeful that they would have.

After all, he was a first-class passenger, one who hadn't even been trapped within the sinking vessel. Surely Victor's body must have been floating somewhere on the surface near the wreckage?

My stomach clenched when we were informed, however, that no, his body was 'never found'. And I did wonder, briefly, if that was indeed true…

But why would the White Star Line lie? Why would they want to withhold someone's body, and bring more desperation onto a grieving widow?

Of course they wouldn't.

And so, as if losing my beloved husband in that horrific manner – after just eighteen months of blissful marriage – wasn't traumatic enough, I was faced with yet another issue. Because, as I later found out, under Spanish law, if there was no body, a person could not be declared legally dead until twenty years after their disappearance.

Which meant my life was to be at a standstill.

No remarrying – not that I would want to – and no inheriting of my husband's fortune – I was grieving… but I cannot rightly say I wouldn't want *that*.

Thankfully, mine and Victor's family all wanted to move on from this. We all needed closure. Lest our grief fester into an infection that would surely poison the rest of our lives.

And so, Victor's family pulled some strings, paid the right people, and before long 'Victor's' body was found.

I cannot say that I am relieved by this outcome. Not yet anyway. The wound of his loss is still too raw.

But one day. One day I am sure I will overcome this tragic event.

Victor gave me everything I had always hoped for in a husband. He was assertive, powerful, funny, and knew what he wanted. And what he wanted was me. All the time. Always.

I am not sure I shall ever find a love like that again. Am not even sure I would want it again if I had the opportunity.

I had wanted to go on the Titanic. Had done nothing more than mention it once or twice over dinner, another time after our regular bout of lovemaking.

Victor had conceded as I knew he would. Had been glad to.

I will have to live with that guilt forever, and I shall. It will be my own secret punishment for having forced his hand.

His mother had warned us not to set foot on a ship.

And I, the new woman in his life, just *had* to oppose her.

9 MONTHS LATER

Edward

God giveth and God taketh away.

It has never before rung so true.

After the Titanic disaster, the Carpathia completed our journey to New York, the 703 survivors plucked from the lifeboats stepping back onto dry land with the greatest relief.

We were saved. We were the lucky ones.

But life would never be the same again.

The ship took with it a devastating amount of life. Sucked entire families into the depths of the Atlantic.

But even those – like us – who had survived, had lost something.

The first thing Ethel and I noticed the loss of – which on the night of the tragedy had not even crossed our minds – was the $300 we had given to a purser at the beginning of our journey, to keep safe. All that money – our life's savings! – just *gone* in an instant.

But we'd remained clearheaded. After all, unlike all those poor lost souls, we had our health and our future. And surely the White Star Line would compensate us for our loss.

We filed a claim, hopeful, but were quickly met with another obstacle. They wanted a receipt of proof that we had entrusted our money to their purser.

A *receipt*! Of *proof*!

Can you believe it?

I was beside myself with fury.

We'd barely escaped with our lives, and now they want a *receipt*! It would have been laughable if it wasn't so infuriating.

To make matters worse, we were offered $20 right then and there in exchange for dropping the claim and promising not to further pursue the matter of our lost money.

But it was more than just money.

That $300 had been the reward for six years of hard work. Six years separated from the woman I wished to marry solely for the purpose of giving her a good life.

And now that life was no longer available to us…

To add insult to injury, Ethel and I had been hounded by news reporters and journalists in the months following the disaster, all desperate to retell our story.

When we were first approached by that officer on the Carpathia, I had bent my version of the story somewhat, much to Ethel's confusion.

I had apologised profusely to her afterwards, but I could not face the shame. I couldn't bear to be remembered as a coward! I told him that I had watched Ethel be made comfortable on the lifeboat. That I had watched it descend, and that I had kept my eyes on her the whole time it was rowing away. I explained that I had jumped into the water as the Titanic was going under, and swum all the way to Ethel's lifeboat, where I was hauled on board by my fellow passengers.

Ethel had corroborated my story, of course. Though she knew nothing of my feelings of dishonour at the time.

But I should have known my lie would not have remained intact for long, for of course, the other passengers on our barge would share their own side of things. And none of them would be able to verify a rescue.

It soon came out that I had not been as heroic as I'd made myself out to have been. That I had, instead, taken a space on a lifeboat that had been intended for a woman, or a child.

But I wasn't the only man aboard our lifeboat, Lawrence Beesley, too, had climbed on shortly after Ethel and I…

Sometimes I wonder if Beesley suffers with this intense survivor's guilt, as I am.

Some nights, I can barely fall asleep! The sound of all those people screaming, dying, still haunts me whenever I close my eyes.

And now we are pariahs, hated by many for the simple fact that we survived when so many others did not.

"We have each other," Ethel would tell me, hoping to quell my woe and devastation.

I remember now how, on one such occasion where she had to be the strong one and coax me out of my melancholy, she had taken my hand and placed it over the growing mound of her belly. And I had pressed my forehead to hers and smiled, a brief moment of happiness in a great sea of misery.

We'd conceived our child on the Titanic, if estimations were to be believed. And for that, at least, our honeymoon had been a blessing.

But now, nine months to the day of the sinking, we are faced with another misfortune. As if we haven't been through enough already…

"How is she?" I ask the doctor now as he takes a seat beside me in the hallway outside Ethel's room.

The doctor offers me a tight-lipped smile, "She is recovering well. Your wife will be fine."

I nod slowly.

"And the baby?" I ask.

That tight-lipped smile again.

"We did what we could," he says, squeezing my shoulder, "But it was a stillbirth."

"So," I say, mulling over my wretched reality, "What was it? The baby?"

The doctor inhales deeply, "A little girl, sir."

I nod again, though I'm not sure I accept this news, *any* of it.

"We would have named her Ethel," I murmur, but the doctor has already risen and is walking away, "Ethel…after her strong and beautiful mother."

And then I drop my head into my hands and weep, the guilt consuming me as it so often did.

Was this my punishment for surviving, when over 1500 others did not?

I don't know how long I sit there, weeping into my hands.

All I know is that, though we may have been some of the lucky ones to leave the tragedy of the Titanic alive, for as long as we shall live, the Titanic tragedy would never leave us.

<u>Author's Note</u>

I want to start off by saying that this book is a work of fiction, the people's personalities and conversations having been entirely invented for the purpose of fluidity in the story.

That being said I would like to make the reader aware that every single person in this book is real, and that everyone mentioned as being on the Titanic (with the exception of James Brown) was a real passenger or crew.

Ethel – I stayed true to Ethel and Edward's story in all things, their recent wedding, their age gap, their controversial engagement, the potential conception of their first child on the Titanic, their tragic stillbirth, Edward's fabricated story upon their rescue, etc.

The only creative liberties I took was in their additional backstories, as there were not many records about those finer details. Edward's past is largely fictitious, as was the death of Ethel's father causing trouble at home before Edward's return from America.

Thomas – Mr Millar's story is almost completely accurate apart from, of course, his thought processes, conversations, and his cause of death, as these are things we will never know for sure. He was indeed involved in the creation of the Titanic, and was widowed shortly before taking the job as Assistant Deck Engineer. His wife Jennie dying of illness and leaving behind a distraught husband and two young sons is also true.

The tale of the two coins given to the boys is real, what Thomas told them – that they must not spend them until his return – is also accurate.

He was one of the many crew members who went down with the ship, remaining at their posts for as long as they could so that the passengers on deck had a chance at survival. Their efforts were heroic, to say the least.

Michel – Wow, what an interesting character to bring to life. Michel Navratil's story really stunned me. He did indeed board the Titanic under the pseudonym Louis Hoffman as he attempted to kidnap his two young sons following a nasty separation from his wife. He really did place his sons on Collapsible D before being lost in the crowd. And it is said that he really did call to his sons that their mother would find them and to tell her that he had always loved her, though this account is disputed since the boys were so young and the event so distressing.

However, I did take creative liberties with his thought processes, of course, as we will never truly know them. I also fictionalised his connection to fellow passenger Victor Peñasco, and his encounter with Mr and Mrs Beane. Though he did lose sight of the boys at one point to play a game of cards with someone who spoke French. His final moment and cause of death was also dramatised.

Catherine – Catherine Nellie Johnston was one of the estimated 50-61 children who died in the sinking of the Titanic. She and her entire family and friends (which was actually a party of 10, including Alice) died on that fateful night.

She was just seven years old, her brother William was nine.

There wasn't much information about their time on the ship, since none survived to tell the tale, which means that their moments spent on the Titanic in this book is largely fictitious. As is their final moment.

But the fact that they postponed their journey to America up to three times before boarding the Titanic is, tragically, true.

Victor – I will admit I had a lot of fun writing this character – and I say character because, though Victor and Maria and Mina were really on the Titanic – I took a lot of creative liberties with Victor's personality.

That being said, his mother really *did* report having a bad feeling about them boarding a ship or boat during their honeymoon and made them swear they would not. It is true that they ignored her warning and that he left his servant behind in Paris to send Victor's mother postcards so that she would not know of their true location at sea.

It is also true that Victor and Maria appeared, by all accounts, to be very much in love.

The account of their separation on that night is true, Maria having been hysterical to be parted from him.

While his final moments, thought processes, and cause of death is fictitious, it is accurate that his body was never recovered, and that his and Maria's family had to go through procedures to be able to move on with their lives.

Harold Cottam – this short account is completely true.

Marcelle – Michel Navratil's wife's narrative is based on her account of things. We will never truly know the full story, but the scandalous divorce, the court case, the temporary separation of parents and sons, the verbal and emotional abuse inflicted on Marcelle is accurate.

The title – I chose the number 1500 as the title of this book to acknowledge those who died in the tragic event. It is generally believed the Titanic sinking to have had *around* 1500 casualties, with the U.S committee suggesting it to have been 1517, the British committee determining 1503, and yet another claiming it was 1534. The sad reality is that we do not know exactly how many souls were lost that night. But with this book, I hope to have brought some of these people's terrifying experiences to light.

They *all*, whether they lived or died, deserve to be remembered.

If you enjoyed this book, please remember to leave a quick review or rating on Amazon or Goodreads.